Murder at Galena Stables

A Karen Prince Mystery

By

Sandra Principe

ISBN: 0-9767954-2-6 (paperback)

Published by: Galena Publishing; PO Box 18; Galena, IL 61036.

Acknowledgements

I would like to thank Tissy Principe for introducing me to the world of horses and horse shows. I would also like to thank my family and friends who read the early version of this book for their time and comments, including: Larry Begun, Barb Alexander, Sara Jean Gray, Lina Haycraft, Lisa Melnick, Laurie Principe, Tissy Principe, Marsha Rinetti, Wanda Ryan, and Carol Seelig.

Disclaimer

Dedication

To my Mother, with much love and gratitude.

Chapter One

Jump Start

The red, yellow and orange stripes of the hot air balloon glowed against the cobalt sky. I squinted into the noon sunlight, trying to make out Marvin Stone and Captain Ed Ballantine in the balloon's tiny basket overhead. It was a glorious Fourth of July here in the country, just outside Galena.

I'm Karen Prince and the handsome fellow seated next to me in the grandstands was Ken Cruise. We were at Galena Stables to see the annual Hunter Jumper Horse Show. This year's opening ceremony featured Marvin, our local veterinarian and parachute enthusiast, jumping from Captain Ed's hot air balloon and landing in the center of the arena.

As we waited for the show to start, I enjoyed the scenery. Galena Stables was nestled in Long Hollow Valley, not far from Eagle Ridge Resort. Tree-covered hills rose around us in every direction. A red tailed hawk, wings spread wide, circled above us, riding the summer thermals. The crowd's chatter filled the air. A three-railed white fence encircled the horse riding ring directly in front of us which had been cleared for this event. There were two other warm-up rings nearby and I could see competitors in them, schooling their horses.

Ken leaned toward my ear and said: "You know, Marvin's been my best friend since grade school. He's always been a bit of a daredevil. On his thirtieth birthday, as a lark, he decided to try parachuting. He's been jumping ever since."

"So, have you stayed in touch your whole lives?" I asked.

"Yup. After high school, we went to UW Madison together then came back here after grad school. Marvin set up his vet practice and I started teaching at Clarke," Ken said.

This hometown connection is one of many things I like about Ken. That, and his smiling blue eyes, strong erect posture, and quick intelligence. Having left my own hometown at the age of seventeen, and then having lived in the anonymity of Chicago most of my adult life, I found Ken's strong community connection comforting.

I trained my binoculars on the hot air balloon's basket and saw a dark form leaning over the side. The horse show announcer's voice boomed: "Here he comes, folks!" Marvin climbed onto the edge of the basket and, without any hesitation, leapt into the air.

All eyes in the arena were now on Marvin Stone. There must have been five hundred spectators who'd come out to see this show. Every one of them, as well as the competitors, stared upward as Marvin's form plummeted toward the ground.

"He'll pull his chute and land himself on that big yellow "X" you see placed in the center of the arena," the announcer said.

The crowd cheered and pointed overhead as Marvin's form grew larger and larger.

"He'll pull that chute cord now, folks," the announcer repeated. We all stared in anticipation.

"He's about 1,000 feet above the ground now. He can steer himself once he opens that chute, folks," the announcer said.

I gave Ken a quizzical glance. He patted my hand.

"He'll pull that rip cord any second," Ken said. "He's just making a dramatic show of it!"

But Marvin continued to fall. The crowd's excited chatter turned to horrified silence and then to screams as Marvin hit the ground. His chute never opened.

"Keep your seats! Please, stay in your seats!" the announcer boomed. But Ken was already on his feet, making his way down from the stands. And I was right behind him.

Just as we got to the fenced arena, the ambulance siren began to wail. I cupped my hands over my ears to dull the sound and made my way through the crowd that had formed around Marvin. The announcer's pleas for people to remain seated hadn't been any more effective than Marvin's parachute. I caught up with Ken and took his hand. We made our way through to Marvin just as the ambulance pulled up alongside the in gate. Marvin's arms and legs were at odd angles and he wasn't moving.

A loud voice behind us commanded, "Step back. Make way. Give us room here." The show's volunteer paramedics, Marcie and JR, moved forward quickly and knelt down, one on each side of Marvin. The crowd pressed in around us. We watched Marcie unbuckle the parachute straps across Marvin's chest. Ken knelt down next to Marcie. I steeled myself and crouched down next to Ken in time to hear him ask: "How's his pulse?"

Marcie shook her head. "I can't find one," she said solemnly. "He's not breathing. I'm starting CPR."

Chapter Two

Who's Who?

As I said, my name is Karen Prince. Five years ago I retired from my Chicago law practice to live and paint in the glorious rolling countryside outside Galena. Folks call Galena "the place that time forgot." And, lucky for us, the glaciers forgot Galena, too. They parted and went around this northwest corner of Illinois three times. As a result, we have hills and valleys, forests, soaring eagles, wild turkeys, an incredible diversity of wildflowers, prairies—well, I could go on. As you can tell, I'm in love with this area. I live quietly, painting the beautiful flowers and keeping a low profile.

Well, I try to keep a low profile. Circumstances seem to have conspired against that. First, through an incredible stroke of luck, I won the Power Ball Lottery and became rich—really, really rich—to the tune of 162 Million Dollars. I know, I know! I couldn't believe it myself! But it happened, and here I am, one of the wealthiest people in the area, if not the entire Midwest.

Most people who win the lottery quit their day jobs. But I'd already done that when I moved out here to paint! And I would never give up the joy I get from creating my floral paintings, so I just keep painting.

I love what I do so much that I had the idea to set up a rather unusual foundation with part of my winnings. It's called Turning Points and its purpose is to help mid-career professionals who want to transition into the arts. Anyway, that's why you might have heard of me. Well, that and the two murders I was involved in—helped solve, I mean!

You see, a few years back, my friend Alice's "ex" turned up dead on her property and I helped find the killer! Then, just this past May, I threw a party on a paddleboat to celebrate the first grant given by my foundation. The party was going along perfectly—until two guests went overboard—literally! That's when I met Ken Cruise.

Ken was the Captain of the Coast Guard boat sent out to look for the guests who'd gone overboard. My then long distance boyfriend was Mark Jordan. Mark was a lawyer, well, is a lawyer, I should say. I mean, he isn't dead, just pretty much out of my life. Mark had been on the paddle boat but he had to get back to Chicago that night—and I haven't seen him since. Abandoning a damsel in distress is definitely against the Prince Charming Code. Anyway, since that fateful paddleboat party I've been spending some time with Ken. He's a perfect gentleman and, I have to say, I enjoy his company. Ken had helped me through the trauma of that May evening and the weeks that followed. It looked like now it was going to be my turn to help him.

We stared at Marcie giving Marvin CPR and willed him to breathe. Ken had his arm around me and whispered in my ear, "You know, I can't believe Marvin's chute didn't open. Marvin is so thorough and precise. I know he would have checked his chute before the jump. He always did."

Marcie stopped CPR, looked up at us and said, "He's gone."

I felt Ken's body tense next to me. "Oh my God," Ken said in a hushed voice I could barely hear.

JR pulled the ambulance into the riding ring and parked right next to Marvin's motionless body. I recognized Joan Marconi, another paramedic, as she climbed out of the ambulance's passenger side and opened the back doors. JR hurried out of the ambulance and helped Joan remove the stainless steel stretcher. They carried it the short distance to Marcie and laid it on the ground next to Marvin's body. We watched in shock as Marcie, JR and Joan lifted Marvin onto the stretcher and placed his body into the back of the ambulance.

Just then, a large, round fellow broke through the growing circle of onlookers. It was Detective Cavanaugh! Detective Cavanaugh had handled those two murder investigations I'd been involved in. We'd gotten to know each other working on those cases, even though Cavanaugh would probably have preferred that I let him handle them alone.

Detective Cavanaugh moved in just as JR was closing the ambulance's back door.

"What happened here?" Cavanaugh demanded.

"Marvin Stone is dead! He jumped out of the hot air balloon and his chute didn't open," JR said.

"Where is his parachute?" Cavanaugh asked. JR looked around. All eyes went to the parachute packet on the ground where Marcie had removed it from Marvin's body. "That's it over there," JR said, pointing to the place of impact.

"We're taking Marvin's body into Galena Hospital," JR said as he started moving toward the front of the ambulance. "The Docs need to pronounce him. All right if we go now?"

"Hang on. Let me see the body before you go," Cavanaugh said. "And no one touch that parachute until I get over there to look at it," Cavanaugh barked at the crowd.

"I'll watch it," Marcie said, moving back over to the abandoned parachute.

Cavanaugh opened the ambulance's rear door again and climbed inside. He reemerged a few minutes later shaking his head. Then he walked over to the parachute. Marcie was standing guard next to it.

Cavanaugh crouched down and lifted what looked like a thin cable. "This rip cord's been cut!" he exclaimed.

"Cut? You mean to say someone intentionally sabotaged Marvin's parachute?" Ken gasped. Cavanaugh's statement sent shock waves through the crowd around him.

Cavanaugh looked up and our eyes met. "You again!" he said. "How come every time a body turns up in Galena you're at the scene, Karen?"

"Oh, believe me, it's not my plan!" I said. "Ken is Marvin's friend. We're here for the horse show and ..." My voice trailed off. And what indeed!

Cavanaugh shouted loudly to no one in particular, "Find that hot air balloon pilot and get him down here, now!" Then he pulled out a small black notebook from his back pocket and wrote down the time, our names and the names of the other people standing next to us in the circle where Marvin's body had been.

"Adam Hall, manager of Galena Stables," a tall thin fellow in jeans said.

"Ox Taylor," the fellow standing next to him told Cavanaugh. "I'm Technical Coordinator for the horse show." Ox was a big fellow, over six feet and probably over two hundred and fifty pounds, most of it muscle. I was guessing that was how he'd gotten his name.

As Detective Cavanaugh took names, the announcer's disembodied voice came over the loudspeaker, "Today's events have been cancelled. The competition will resume tomorrow morning at 9 a.m."

Most of the spectators had already left their seats. Now that there wasn't going to be a horse show, the rest of them streamed down.

"I think I'd like to go home," Ken said, quietly.

"Do you want me to come with you?" I asked.

7

"No. Thanks, but I'd like to be alone for a little while," he responded.

We'd driven our own cars to the horse show. We'd expected to leave separately—just not like this.

"O.K.," I said. "Give me a call when you feel like talking."

"I will," Ken said. He leaned over, gave my forehead a kiss and headed out. I watched his back as he blended into the exiting crowd.

A wave of loneliness washed over me. The shock was starting to let other feelings through. Although Ken wanted to be alone, I definitely did not. I knew Polly was here somewhere and I wanted to find her.

Polly is Polly Andrews. She's one of my country neighbors and a good friend. We met when I moved out here, even though we'd both lived and worked in Chicago for years. In fact, Polly still does. She's a public relations phenom, with her own PR firm in Chicago's Loop. On weekends, Polly rides horses here at Galena Stables and was supposed to be one of today's exhibitors. Since most of the exhibitors were taking their horses back to the stables, I figured I'd look for Polly there.

I joined the flow of riders and their families leaving the competition area. Once we were past the riding rings, a dirt road running next to the Apple River led to the stable area. Some folks were riding their horses at a slow pace, some people were walking and, much to my surprise, quite a few people were in golf carts. I suppose the carts were a good idea, actually. This whole set-up was about a mile long, from the parking area to the far end where the stables were located. It would be a lot easier and faster to get around in a golf cart than walking.

The road was wide enough to accommodate carts going in each direction. As we moved along in a slow procession, I noticed that most of the exhibitors were teenage girls, young women in their early twenties, or women in their forties, probably returning to the sport of their youth. There were a few men, but not many.

Polly and I had talked about the horse show just yesterday. She'd told me that the exhibitors on this circuit spend their year traveling around the country from horse show to horse show. Parents travel with the younger competitors and spend a bundle doing it. Polly estimated that being on the circuit could cost up to $5,000 per week, per horse, plus living and traveling expenses. These folks were the rich and famous you see in fancy horse magazines. They also appeared to be strong, disciplined and serious about their sport. No joking and jostling here. Even the youngest girls looked intense. I suppose riding a twelve hundred pound animal over jumps requires serious attention. And, of course, the sight we'd just seen had certainly sobered everyone.

According to Polly, every few weeks these riders and their families were in a new city. The technical coordinator and his crew arrive a week in advance and create a virtual village for the horse show, complete with electric and water hookups for the exhibitors' RV's; stalls for the horses; riding rings, jumps and judging stands; a sound system covering the whole area; as well as a computerized office to handle registration, show entries and imputing class results. Polly had described it as a high-end traveling circus coming to town. The horse show folks moved from town to town in hundred thousand dollar motor homes with horse trailers hauling horses worth thousands of dollars. This was quite an exclusive mobile world.

A five minute walk brought me to the stables. There were the temporary stalls, which had been created just for this event, and the permanent Galena Stables. The temporary stalls had a metal frame, covered with canvas walls, roofing and awnings. As I walked by, I couldn't believe how elaborately some of these horse stalls were decorated. There were sitting rooms with canvas chairs and photos of horses. Blue, red, yellow and white winner's ribbons were hung around the entrances. Hundreds of potted evergreens and flowering plants had been brought in to create gardens around the stalls' entrances. It was quite an elaborate sight, all the more impressive when you considered that none of this had been here two weeks ago!

Just past the temporary stalls, I came to the white wooden barn with tall green letters over the door announcing, "Galena Stables." I'd been here before to watch some of Polly's riding events. The building contained an indoor riding ring as well as the permanent horse stalls. This was where the local Galena competitors housed their horses and where I hoped to find Polly. And sure enough, I did.

Polly was at the side of the schooling area talking to Sassie Ballantine and some other local riders. Polly is a striking blonde, in perfect shape and always exquisitely dressed. Sassie is another great local horsewoman. She's the heir to the Sassafrass Root Beer fortune and is married to Captain Ed, the hot air balloon pilot.

As I walked up to Polly, Sassie, and the others in their group, I was struck by Sassie's exotic look. She is about five foot ten, with a horsewoman's lean strong muscles, glowing olive skin, dark almond shaped eyes and long dark brown hair that had been plaited back for the horse show. When Sassie wasn't riding, she wore her long, curly hair loose in a Methuselah-like halo. Polly broke from the circle and gave me a hug, punctuated by air kisses to both cheeks.

"Karen, it's so good to see you. But we're all in shock about Marvin. What a horrible, horrible accident! We were all just talking about it," Polly said. Polly took my hand and guided me into the circle of people, saying, "Karen, let me introduce you to everyone. Everyone, this is my friend, Karen Prince. Karen, you know Sassie, I think?"

"Yes, of course," I said, smiling at Sassie.

"Hi, Karen," Sassie said.

"And this is Harry Henry," Polly said, indicating a short, stocky fellow in a blue tee shirt, jeans and a cowboy hat. "Harry's a trainer here at the stables." Harry's face and arms had the look of old tanned leather. He'd either seen a lot of sun, or led a rough life, or both. Harry had thick light brown hair that tickled his collar. A black and tan hound dog sat quietly at his heels.

Harry and I exchanged nods and half smiles to acknowledge both the introduction and the somber circumstances.

"And this is Red Hamish. Red's a trainer from Charleston," Polly said. Red was about six feet tall, with an athletic build. He had closely cropped red hair which set off his pale face and blue eyes. Arched red eyebrows gave him a quizzical expression. He had that *au currant* facial hair I'd never grown accustomed to, where his moustache connected with a close cropped beard covering just his chin. Red was in well fitting jeans, a pale blue oxford shirt and black riding boots. I shook his extended hand.

"And I think you know Brie," Polly said, continuing her introductions around the circle. Well, I knew of Brie Kellen. Who in Galena didn't? I'd seen her photo in the Galena Gazette often enough. Brie had the look of a disgruntled Viking Goddess. She is six foot two inches tall, with straight blonde hair falling below her shoulders, ice blue eyes and a lean body that looked like it had been chiseled out of marble. She held Puff, her white, long-haired Chihuahua, in the crook of her arm. Word was that Brie had bought Puff to console herself when Marvin had broken off their relationship last year to date Tara Trilling. Within six months, Tara Trilling had become Tara Stone.

Puff barked in the classic Chihuahua tonal range, somewhere between whistling tea pot and blaring fire alarm. Brie pressed the little dog to her cheek without smiling and hissed, "Shh! Puff! Shh!"

Brie wore a pink oxford shirt and tan riding pants. There was no smile, no extended hand. Brie's reputation for moodiness was well deserved. Polly moved on with her introductions around the circle.

"And this is Carl Castoni," Polly said, indicating a handsome young man in his mid-twenties. Carl was of medium height, with dark brown, neatly cropped hair, a clean shaven face and a ready smile. He wore a bright red polo shirt and blue jeans.

"A pleasure to meet you," Carl said, quickly extending his hand to me.

"Carl is filling in as the horse show vet while Marvin is— was..." Polly's voice trailed off.

"I offered to fill in for Marvin while he parachuted," Carl said. "The horse show has to have a vet in attendance at all times."

"Of course," I said. That makes sense. A movement behind Carl caught my eye. I looked over Carl's shoulder and was momentarily confused. Polly must have sensed my confusion because she turned to follow my gaze, then chuckled and said, "Oh, here comes Clay, Carl's twin brother."

"Thank heavens," I said. "For a minute there, I thought I was seeing things!"

Clay joined our circle and stood next to his brother. Even standing side by side, it was difficult to tell them apart. Same dark brown eyes, close cropped curly brown hair and full smiles. They were even in the same red shirt. That's when I noticed the words "Castoni Vineyards" embroidered on their shirt pockets.

"Are you vintners?" I asked, after the introductions.

"That's my field, so to speak," Clay said with a small chuckle. "I leave the horses to my brother, here," Clay said, putting his arm around Carl's shoulders. "While Carl was in veterinary school, I planted vineyards. We produced our first bottling last fall," Clay said, with pride.

"It's great wine," Sassie volunteered.

"I think wine-making is fascinating!" I said.

"I'd be happy to give you a tour of our operations sometime," Clay offered. "In fact, we're having a special event at the vineyard after the horse show closes on Monday. Bring a friend and join us," Clay said.

"Thank you. I'd love to do that," I said, returning his smile.

"Invite Ken," Polly suggested. "We can all go together."

"Excellent idea," Clay said. We'll plan on the three of you joining us. Starts at 7:00 p.m. to give everyone time to clean up after the horse show," Clay said.

"Is everyone else here coming?" Carl asked.

"Ed and I are, Sassie said.

"I'll be there," Harry said.

"Wouldn't miss a chance to taste the local wines!" Red said.

"I'll be there, too," Brie said, levelly.

Our conversation was interrupted by the ring of a cell phone. "Excuse me," Sassie said as she pulled her phone from her pocket and stepped away from the circle. She returned in a minute and said, "I have to leave. I've been trying to reach Ed. They've landed and stowed the balloon and I'm going to meet him at home. He must be in shock after this."

"I think Detective Cavanaugh is talking to him, too," I said.

"Detective Cavanaugh?" Sassie asked. "Why?"

"Haven't you all heard?" I asked, surprised. I could tell by their blank stares that they hadn't.

"Well, Detective Cavanaugh said Marvin's parachute rip cord had—well, it'd been cut!" I said.

Everyone gasped. "Cut! You mean someone intended to kill Marvin!" Sassie said.

"Intended to and did," I said.

"Are you sure?" Polly asked.

"I was there when Cavanaugh found the cut rip cord," I said.

"Who would have done that?" Brie shouted.

The seven of us looked at her. Brie had an obvious motive. She'd been angry and obsessed with Marvin for the past year and everyone knew it. Still, no one said a thing to her.

"I'd better find Ed right now," Sassie said. "I don't think Ed knows that Marvin's rip cord was cut, yet. Excuse me, everyone," Sassie said and abruptly left.

"You know, I need to go too," Polly said. "Please excuse us, everyone. Can you come back with me to Angel's stall for a minute?" Polly asked, giving me a very intent look.

"Sure," I answered. "Nice to meet you all," I said, looking around the circle at Brie, Harry, Red and the Castoni brothers.

I followed Polly down a dark wooden hallway that led from the riding ring to the stable area. In about one hundred feet, the hallway came to a tee. Polly led us to the right. Before we turned, I glanced down the left passageway and saw a shadowed figure in the distance. Whoever it was saw me look at him but made no acknowledgment. And he was out of sight in a flash as I turned right to follow Polly. She has a determined stride and I hurried to keep pace with her.

"That other corridor leads to the original stalls. Galena Stables expanded last year. Angel's in the new addition, this way," Polly said.

There were horse stalls on either side of us now but, glancing around, I didn't see any other people. I took the opportunity of being out of earshot of the others to get Polly's take on what had happened today.

"Did Marvin have any enemies that would do this?" I asked.

"Well, I could speculate about who and why," she whispered back to me.

"Really? Care to share your ideas?" I asked.

"Sure. I'll tell you what I've heard," Polly said, slowing her pace and leaning toward me a bit. "But let's talk when we get to Angel's stall." I raised my eyebrows. Apparently Polly was concerned about someone in the stables overhearing us!

A few more stalls and we were there. Angel is a big, black, beautiful mare, and Polly's pride and joy. "Good girl," Polly cooed as she opened the stall door and slid in. She waited for me to come in as well and closed the stall's half-door behind me. Polly grabbed the grooming brush and brushed Angel's already shiny coat as she said, "For the last month, rumors have been flying about Marvin and Sassie. They've been meeting a lot—without Tara and Ed. Galena is a very small place and so is the horse world—neither is a good place to conduct a secret tryst."

"So, you think Marvin and Sassie were having an affair?" I asked, shocked.

"I don't know for sure," Polly said. "I only know Marvin was spending a lot of time with Sassie. And there was a lot of talk about it around here. You know, both Tara and Captain Ed would have had the opportunity to cut that parachute rip cord. And they both would have had a motive if they thought they were being cheated on," Polly said.

"They were all practically newlyweds!" I gasped.

"I know, I know. But that might make them even more upset if they thought something was going on. And stranger things have been known to happen," Polly said, looking at me with a knowing expression.

Chapter Three

Run For It!

"I can't imagine Captain Ed killing anyone, let alone Marvin. You don't actually think he's responsible, do you?" I asked Polly.

"Oh, I don't know. They were alone up there in that balloon. Maybe Captain Ed pretended to help Marvin adjust his chute and cut the pull cord while he was doing that," Polly said.

"But why would Captain Ed jeopardize everything he has? His home, his fortune, his marriage?" I asked.

"Maybe he felt he was protecting those things, not jeopardizing them. I mean, if Captain Ed thought Marvin was having an affair with Sassie, he might have been desperate to stop it," Polly said. "In fact, just yesterday I heard that Marvin and Sassie were having lunch at Eagle Ridge," Polly continued.

"Lunch at Eagle Ridge is hardly sneaking around," I countered. "It's about as public as you can get."

"Well, my source says they were laughing and whispering and drinking wine," Polly reported.

"Your source? Now who is that?" I asked. Polly just looked at me. "Well, it sounds to me like they might just be friends," I said. I felt defensive on behalf of Captain Ed and Sassie. And Marvin too.

"Well, Sassie grew up extremely wealthy, you know. Sometimes that makes people feel entitled to get whatever they want. And maybe Sassie wanted Marvin," Polly said. "In fact, the more I think about it, that could have been exactly what happened. Carl said he heard Sassie and Ed arguing in the arena yesterday."

"Did I hear my name?" a deep voice called from the doorway and startled Polly and me.

We both turned abruptly and saw Carl Castoni leaning over the stall's half-door looking in at us.

"Oh, Carl," Polly said. "You startled me. I was just telling Karen about the conversation you overheard yesterday between Captain Ed and Sassie."

Carl leaned into the stall. "If that was a conversation, I'd hate to see an argument," Carl said, raising his dark eyebrows.

"What were they arguing about?" I asked.

"Ed was upset about Sassie's taking a trip without him. Sassie's planning to go to Asheville next week and Ed didn't know about it until he heard a message on their answering machine confirming her registration."

"Asheville! She must be going to the Biltmore Summer Classic. Bella and I will be there too. I'm flying down on Thursday. My Aunt Tissy hired Bella to cater the Grand Prix dinner at the Asheville horse show. This will be Bella's first big catering event outside Galena and I want to be there to see it. My foundation's grant helped Bella start her new career in catering, so I feel a special pride and responsibility for Bella's success. But I didn't know Sassie was going, too" I said.

"Well, apparently neither did Ed," Carl said.

"But Sassie's going to a horse show doesn't sound like a big deal to me," I added.

"Well, it shouldn't be—if she were going alone," Polly said, pointedly.

We both looked at her.

"Are you saying you think she was planning to meet Marvin there?" I asked.

"There, or maybe somewhere on the way," Polly said.

"Polly, do you know that for a fact or are you just hypothesizing?" I asked. It was one thing to spin stories to create buzz about some product in Chicago. But we were talking about real people and someone could very easily get hurt by that kind of talk.

"O.K., O.K. I was just speculating. But it fits with what I've been seeing and hearing around here," Polly said.

"Well, be careful about feeding the rumor mill," I said. "We want to get to the truth and it won't help if wild stories start spreading."

Suddenly there was a loud boom that shook the rafters. I let out an inadvertent scream and looked over at Polly. She was as stunned as I was. Thunder echoed around us. "That was close!" I said.

"Really close!" Polly said.

"Wow!" Carl said putting his hands over his ears. "It was clouding over when I was outside a minute ago, but according to the weather-guessers it wasn't supposed to rain so soon! They said this wasn't coming until this evening."

Another crash of thunder reverberated through the stable. Angel threw her head back, whinnied and stomped her hooves. Apparently, Angel didn't like lightning any better than I did.

Polly cooed soothing words to Angel and stroked her neck. "It's all right, girl. It's out there. We're safe in here." This time I hoped Polly was right.

"That's odd," Carl said. "Do you smell something?"

I looked at him. Of course I smelled something. We were in a stable. But I didn't think that was what Carl was talking about.

He looked quizzically at Polly and sniffed the air, squinching up his nose. "Karen, come out here and tell me what you smell," he said, looking around him.

I came out of the stall and stood next to Carl. There was the faintest whiff of—smoke! I looked at Carl and we locked eyes. "I smell it," I said, now deadly serious. We both looked down the corridor. The horses farther down the way must have smelled it too, because they were naying and kicking their stall doors. Polly looked at us.

"I smell smoke, Polly. I'm going down the hall to see what it is," I said and took off at a jog, back the way we'd entered. Carl was sprinting right next to me. As we got closer to the split in the hallways, the scent of smoke got stronger and stronger. I looked down the cross corridor and saw smoke drifting from one of the far stalls.

"Oh my God!" I gasped, and then screamed, "Fire!" at the top of my lungs. Red Hamish, Harry Henry and Clay Castoni came running to see what was going on. When they saw the smoke they joined in yelling "Fire." Panic filled the air as palpably as the smoke. Other riders quickly appeared and led their frightened horses outside.

Someone pulled a fire alarm and the piercing sound made speech impossible. I'm not a horse person but I knew I had to help get the horses out of the stable. Carl saw my fear and yelled, "Just open the stall doors. The horses know their way out." I swallowed my fear, opened the nearest stall and let the horse run free. Someone would have to round them up outside. Now the thing was to get the horses—and ourselves—out of here!

Carl ran towards the source of the fire and opened the rest of the stalls on that side of the stable. Between the alarm, the smoke and the commotion, the place was in chaos. Polly ran by with Angel in tow. I finished opening the last of the stalls on my side and ran outside, right into the pouring rain. Ox had just pulled up with a water truck. I banged on the driver's door to get his attention and yelled, "Come on this way." He nodded and I took off toward the far side of the stable. When we rounded the corner, Carl flagged the truck toward the burning stall.

Stable hands and riders were all running to catch the horses we'd let out. Lightning pierced the air and thunder boomed around us. Ox and his crew sprayed water into the burning stall. I watched the water arc from the hose in through the open door. Within ten minutes, Ox had the fire contained.

"Whose stall is that?" I asked one of the riders standing in the crowd watching the smoldering structure.

"Brie's!" he said. I looked around for her, but neither Brie nor her horse were anywhere to be seen.

It was only about 4:00 p.m., but it had already been a long, long day. I was soaking wet and I just wanted to be home. I looked around for Polly but couldn't find her in all the commotion. The adrenaline rush that had propelled me into action during the fire now left me drained. Time to go.

Chapter Four

Seeing Red

Half walking, half jogging, I headed for the parking lot where I'd left my little silver convertible, the Boxster. Thank heavens I'd put the top up when I parked!

The temperature must have dropped twenty degrees since I'd arrived here nearly five hours ago. Rain ran down my neck making me shiver. I was chilled to the bone.

The temporary stalls came into view on my right and I decided to duck in for a moment's shelter. I couldn't afford to get sick now. I had to finish *"Orchid in Morning Light,"* the painting I promised my New York gallery for their upcoming September show. Plus, I was giving the introduction at the Antique Art Show tomorrow afternoon at the Galena Historical Society.

I pushed the canvas flap aside and walked into the tented temporary stalls. The canvas sides and roof strained against the wind but they kept the rain out. I looked into each of the stalls as I passed by them—nosy me! Red Hamish, the trainer Polly had just introduced me to, was in the third stall. He was standing with four of his riders, probably making sure his clients and their horses were all accounted for after the fire. He looked up and I must have been quite a sight because he said, "Karen, are you all right? Come on in and dry off."

"Thanks," I said. "I'm fine. I'm just cutting through here on the way to my car."

"Don't be silly. This summer storm will pass as quickly as it came up. Wait it out in here with us."

The dry stable did look a lot better than the weather outside. And I guessed it wouldn't matter if I got home a little later. "Maybe that is a good idea. Thanks," I said and joined their circle.

"Karen, let me introduce you to my riders. This is Michelle, Kristy, Jennifer, Jessica, and Anna."

"Nice to meet you," I said. "Where are you all from?"

"Charleston," Red responded, on behalf of the girls, who looked somewhat shy. I'm not good at guessing ages, but I thought they were about sixteen.

"You're all a long way from home," I replied.

"Oh, we travel all across the country for these shows. Don't we girls?" Red said, looking around the circle at the five young women in identical pink oxford blouses, tan riding pants and knee-high black boots. These young women must have already been inside when the rain started because none of them were wet, which made me even more conscious of my dripping state. As if reading my mind, Red went to one of the trunks and pulled out a blanket. "Here, put this around you. You look cold," he said.

"Thanks, I am," I said, gladly accepting the red wool blanket. It was probably a horse blanket but it sure felt good around my shoulders. I ran my fingers through my hair and pushed some of the water out of it.

"Is everyone in your group all right after that fire?" I asked.

"Yes, Ma'am. We were all finished riding and we'd come back here when we heard the alarm and folks yelling 'fire,' " Kristy said. She was the tallest and seemed to speak for the group.

"Any idea how that fire could have started?" I asked.

"Could have been the lightning," Red said.

"Or maybe some crazy person started it," Michelle said. The other girls looked at her.

"Or it could have been an accident," Anna added.

Michelle's comment made me wonder if they knew something more about the fire than they'd said so far. The shadowy image of the figure I'd seen earlier in the stable came flooding back to me.

"Did any of you young ladies see anything suspicious?" I asked, looking around the circle.

They looked at each other, shook their heads and responded in unison, "No, Ma'am,"

Jessica, the shortest of the girls, was standing facing the hallway. She nudged Anna, standing next to her. I followed their gaze and saw a scrawny, long haired young man in jeans leading a large black horse into the stall across from us.

Red must have seen him then too because he yelled, "Hey! You can't put that horse in there." Red's shout mixed with the sounds of the wind and rain. The young man seemed oddly oblivious to the commotion around him.

Red strode to the hallway and yelled again, "Hey, fella! Stop! That's not your stall. That's Pine Top Farm's stall."

The young man was in a major stupor. He turned toward us, his eyes hidden beneath long curly bangs. "I, ah, I'm supposed to bring Elvis back, ah, back to his stall," he stammered.

"Well, that's not his stall, is it?" Red asked.

Before the young man could answer, Harry Henry came running up to him. "Bring that horse back around this way and stay there with him. Get him some water, too," Harry said, looking at the lather on the horse's neck.

Harry looked into our stall, nodded to us, and was off at quite a clip. The young man followed, leading the glistening black horse down the hall, away from us.

The girls looked at each other and raised their eyebrows.

"Who was that odd fellow with Harry?" I asked Red.

"I take it he's one of Harry's stable hands," he said. "That was Brie's horse. I suppose they're looking for a temporary stall for him after the fire," Red said.

"Do any of you know that young man?" I asked.

They shook their heads in the negative. "No," Kristy said. "But he's been hanging around and watching us ride."

Red spoke up. "I haven't met him myself, but I did ask some of the local riders about him. As Kristy said, he's been hanging around my riders a lot. His name is Norman Trout. I hear he used to work with the vet and now he does odd jobs around the stables."

"Which vet did he work for?" I asked.

"Marvin Stone, the parachute fellow that was killed," Red said.

"He worked for Marvin? Why did he stop?" I asked.

"Don't know," Red said. "I didn't hear that part of the story."

The rain sounded like it was letting up. I noticed because Harry was walking by again and I could distinctly hear him as he said, "I'm talking about Goldie."

"Hey, Harry," Red said to him. "Got a minute? We have a question here."

Harry looked over at the group of us and said, "Sure." He turned back to the young man who was still following him, this time without the black horse, and said "Go get Goldie and put her in the stall next to Elvis. You got that?"

"Yep," Norman said, and shuffled off, shoulders slouched, feet dragging.

"Man! You'd think he'd have enough sense to get a sick horse out of that smoke without being told," Harry said to Red, when he joined our circle.

"Whose horse is sick?" Red asked.

"Brie's new horse, Goldie. She was a good horse too. I found her for Brie about a month ago. And Goldie was doing just fine until Marvin got hold of her," Harry said.

"What happened?" Red asked.

"She's near lame, is what's happened. I don't think she'll ever jump again. All 'cause of that vet," Harry said. Harry adjusted his black hat and met Red's stare.

"Are you saying Goldie is lame because of Marvin?" I asked.

"That's the sum of it," Harry said. "Oh, Marvin tried to cover it up. He blamed Norman, even fired him! But it's obvious that Marvin did something to that horse," Harry said.

"I don't follow. Why did Marvin fire Norman?" I asked.

"That was just a cover-up. That's what Brie and I figured out. That's why Brie hired Norman as a stable hand. Guy is dumb as a box, I'll admit. But Brie felt sorry for him having to take the heat for Marvin."

Wow! If Brie blamed Marvin for her horse being lame, could that have pushed her anger with Marvin over the edge? But making Norman a scapegoat just didn't sound like the Marvin I knew. I'd seen Marvin over the years when he'd taken care of my cat, Truffles. Marvin was always polite and competent. And besides, he was Ken's friend. I was sure that if Marvin had been responsible for Goldie's condition, he would have said so. I didn't know why Marvin had fired Norman, but I was pretty sure it wasn't to pass the blame for his own actions. I let the subject drop and said, "I heard the fire started in Brie's stall. Has anyone here heard what caused the fire?"

"Not for sure," Harry said. "But it looks like a lightning strike."

"Is Brie all right?" I asked.

"I think so. But I haven't actually seen her. She's ..." Harry's answer was cut short.

"She's right here," Brie said as she walked into the stall carrying Puff in her arms. "Where is Elvis?" Brie asked Harry. Brie either knew everyone in our circle or wasn't bothering with introductions. My money was on the latter.

"He's in one of the spare temporary stalls, down the way there," Harry said, pointing in the direction he'd come from. "I just sent Norman over to bring back Goldie."

"You know, he was supposed to have Elvis back in his stall when that fire started," Brie said. "So I suppose it's a good thing Norman is always late."

"Or else Elvis would have been in there when the fire started?" I gasped.

"I'm just glad no one was hurt," Red said, trying to keep a calm atmosphere for his riders.

"We all are, I'm sure," I said. "And now that the storm's ended, I'm going to head home. I'm still sopping wet!"

"I think I'd like to get out of these clothes too," Brie said, looking down at a tiny splatter of mud on her black boots. I wondered how in the world she had managed to stay so clean and dry.

We said our goodbyes and I made my way back along the Apple River. I passed the now deserted riding arenas and went out the exit gate. I found my little silver sports car waiting for me, one of the last cars in the Visitors' Parking Area. I started the engine, then pressed the "bat-mobile" button and watched the black fabric top magically fold back on its own. I remembered the cardigan sweater I kept folded behind the driver's seat. Excellent! I pulled it out, shrugged into it, and buttoned it up tight. I covered my wet hair with the blue and red Cubs baseball cap I keep in the center console, cranked up the heat, set the electric seats on high and pulled out of the lot. I know, I know, not the most energy efficient move, nor the best way to stay warm, but what's the point of having a convertible if you don't put the top down?

Watching the countryside fly by couldn't erase the day's events, but it helped dim the memory for a few minutes. The Boxster gripped the road as I leaned into the curves. Clark Lane ran into Long Hollow Road then followed a ridge over to Highway 20. The vistas along the way were spectacular. Light streamed through the breaking clouds. Red Angus cattle grazed on the glistening green hillsides. Corn and soybean fields made a patchwork quilt of the rolling hills. Broad leafed oak and hickory forests formed a backdrop to the farmed land. I lost myself in the passing scenery and arrived on Blackjack Road and back home just before 6:00 p.m.

Truffles, my black Norwegian Forest cat, greeted me as I came through the door. She raised her fluffy tail and trilled as she circled around my ankles. I bent down and scooped her up in my arms. "Glad to see you too!" I cooed at her.

"Time to feed me!" her insistent meows said loud and clear. We marched to the kitchen together, where I fed Truffs and nuked myself a restorative cup of hot chocolate. What was it about chocolate that made it so wonderful? Maybe it was the combination of sugar, caffeine and fat——one of those was bound to perk you up!

Next, I steamed myself in a hot shower and then put on my most comfy cashmere sweats. Wow, that was better. Braced by the shower and hot chocolate, I called Ken to see how he was doing. The answer was, not well. But who could blame him. He'd just seen his best friend killed. My heart went out to him. This kind man had experienced such loss: three years ago his wife, and now his best friend. Ken was being pretty much non-communicative. I guess, like a lot of men, he went into his "cave" when he was upset and just wanted to be left alone. I obliged, mostly because I had no idea what to say, and suggested that we talk the next day. It was so awful. I felt anger rising in me, anger, and an overpowering desire for justice. I wanted to know who'd killed Marvin and I wanted that person brought to justice.

Right then and there I determined I would do whatever I could to find Marvin's killer. I thought of how many people had been hurt by the killer's horrendous actions: Ken; Marvin's widow, Tara; and Marvin's extended family and friends. And there were the riders and the folks in the audience who'd never forget that gruesome sight. Marvin had cared for so many of our townsfolk's' pets. He'd touched a lot of people's lives. He'd been such an important part of our community; someone had to know who'd killed Marvin. And I was going to find out, too.

I decided to stop in at the veterinary clinic when it opened on Monday, assuming Carl opened the clinic. But I expected he would. Animals still needed care. And maybe someone at the clinic would have an idea about who might have been angry with Marvin. And tomorrow I'd see a lot of people at the Galena Historical Society event. Maybe I could get some leads there. Which reminded me, I still had to prepare my opening comments for the Historical Society's Antique Art Show tomorrow afternoon. I had to get on that now. Oh Jeeze! Why do I procrastinate on things like this?

I got out a legal pad, a habit I'd developed in my former life, and started making notes. We'd based the format for the event on the PBS program: Antiques Road Show. We had a panel of four art experts, including yours truly. Anyone who wanted to could bring in a painting and our panel would do its best to give the painting's owner information about the artist and the work. It would be fun to see the paintings people brought in for identification.

All I had to do was make the opening remarks, give a little background on the Historical Society's own treasured painting, "Peace in Union," and be on the panel. I read through the Historical Society's brochures and learned that "Peace in Union" measures nine feet by twelve feet; is an oil painting on canvas, and was presented by Judge E. W. Kohlsaat of Chicago, on behalf of his brother, H. H. Kohlsaat, on the seventy-fifth anniversary of General Grant's birth. The painting is by Thomas Nast and depicts Lee's surrender to Grant at Appomattox in 1865. I did the math and figured that since Grant was born in 1822, the painting was presented in 1897, five years before Nast's death.

The painting features a near life-size rendering of General Grant, standing in front of a dozen high ranking Union officers. Grant is shaking hands with General Lee, who is standing with two of his own officers. I fired up my laptop and read about Nast on-line in the Encyclopedia Britannica. It turned out that Thomas Nast was a famous political cartoonist for Harper's Weekly. Among other things, he created the Republican Party's elephant. Nast was a strong Union supporter and his political cartoons against slavery prompted President Lincoln to call Nast, "our greatest recruiting sergeant." Interesting.

I also did a bit of research about the Union officers depicted in the painting. One of the more interesting side stories was that of Ely S. Parker. Parker was a full blooded Seneca Indian, who was the Construction Superintendent for the Galena Post Office. The construction took place under the auspices of the Office of Construction, Treasury Department, from 1857 through 1859. So Parker must have been hired by them. Mr. Parker later became a Major-General on General Grant's staff during the Civil War. After Grant was elected President, he appointed Parker Commissioner of Indian Affairs in 1869.

Galena prides itself on its association with General Grant. With a little help from Google, I learned that Grant had moved to Galena in 1860. His father had a leather shop on Main Street. In 1861 Grant accompanied the first volunteers to Springfield. Upon Grant's return to Galena in 1865 after the war, the people of Galena presented General Grant with a beautiful three story red brick home on Bouthillier Street. It was in Galena that Grant heard the results of his election to the office of President of the United States. The Grant home is now an Illinois state historic site and is open as a tourist attraction. These connections keep Grant's memory alive and well in Galena to this day.

When I'd gone over my remarks, I checked the time: 8:00 p.m. I still had an hour before even an "early to bed, early to rise" person, such as myself, could respectably tuck in for the night. Since I still had my computer on, I made my room reservations at the Biltmore Inn in Asheville for next week. With a few clicks I had a hotel room, car rental, and driving directions from the airport to the Biltmore. I'm just old enough that I am still amazed at the things I can do with this little computer! It certainly makes life in the country a lot more interesting.

I poured myself a wee bit of Macallan's scotch and sipped it in my chaise lounge with Truffs on my lap. When I'd finished my nightcap I tucked in and was asleep as soon as my head hit the pillow.

Chapter Five

Orchid Day

I awoke at 8:30 Sunday morning to the call of my fifty-two orchid plants. Well, all right, they didn't actually "call" to me. But I do awake each Sunday with them on my mind. That's because Sunday is the time for their weekly care: watering, fertilizing, repotting when necessary and, of course, praising them for their spectacular blooms. Yes, I do believe in talking to my plants! In exchange for their weekly care, each orchid produces a phenomenal arc of flowers which lasts for months. And, as an added bonus, they're the perfect models for my paintings. In fact, there's a nearly completed orchid painting on my easel right now.

Orchids have an undeserved reputation for being difficult to grow. I'll admit they are particular in their care requirements. But once you understand their unique needs, they're really not difficult at all.

Essentially, an orchid grower has to simulate an orchid's natural environment. That includes regular tropical rains. So each plant must be gently carried to the sink and given a shower from the sprayer. Then, the plant must be allowed to sit undisturbed for ten minutes or so, while it soaks up all the moisture it can. This is followed by a second watering with very dilute fertilizer. Then each orchid is returned to its usual spot, preferably near a window.

Orchids are epiphytes. They have air roots that hold them to the sides of trees. They don't draw nutrition from the trees, just physical support and shelter. That's why, unlike typical house plants which are potted in soil, orchids are potted in a special mix of bark, peat and porous material such as lava or perlite. In the Midwest, perlite is easier to come by than lava. Most orchids prefer that their roots dry out between weekly waterings. Using a porous pot and this special potting mix accomplishes that quite easily.

Orchids are adapted to the filtered light they would receive through the tree leaves. In a home setting, east light is said to simulate this best. However, my orchid collection has expanded well beyond the capacity of my east facing windows. Happily, I find they often do just as well in north, west and south facing windows, as long as they don't receive too much direct summer sun. So, those are the conditions I try to simulate for my orchids. And they respond with an array of white, purple, yellow and lavender flowers.

Oh, I almost forgot! The final component in getting orchids to bloom is a sharp temperature change between day and night. My orchid books suggest a twenty degree differential. I don't get quite that in my home but I must come pretty close. I expect keeping the plants near the windows intensifies the daytime temperatures and the result is that I have orchids in bloom all year round.

As I carried pots to and from the sink, shower and tub, Truffles watched the plant parade from the comfort of my bedroom chaise lounge. We both listened to Pam Ohms's ethereal harp music float from the CD player. Pam is a local harpist with two wonderful CD's: Praise and Celebration. I love them both—the perfect music for a Sunday morning.

I was just finishing the last of my orchids when the phone rang. Caller ID announced "Ken Cruise." I had just picked up a dripping orchid pot from the sink and scurried to return it to its place on my bedroom plant table. Skidding to a stop in my stocking feet, I picked up the phone just before the answering machine kicked in.

"Hi, Ken. Just a minute," I said breathily and placed the phone next to the receiver on my nightstand.

I picked up Truffs, who had pranced over to the phone as soon as it rang. For some reason, whenever I talk on the phone, Truffs likes to curl up in my lap. Maybe she thinks I'm talking to her. Or maybe she just knows its one of the few times I am likely to sit still. In any event, she seems to enjoy being part of my phone conversations. I settled myself on the bed, placed Truffs in my lap and returned the phone to my ear.

"O.K. I'm all settled. How are you?" I asked.

"Could be better. How about you?" Ken replied.

I filled Ken in on the events at Galena Stables after he'd left: the storm, the fire, and then, as gently as I could, I told him the rumors about Marvin and Sassie having an affair.

"That's absolutely ridiculous!" Ken said. "Marvin and Tara were very much in love."

"Was there anything you noticed? Any sign of trouble between them?" I asked.

"No!" Ken replied emphatically. "They were great together. Sure, there was an age difference. But that didn't matter to either of them," Ken said. "In fact, Marvin was planning a surprise birthday party for Tara. Sassie and Ed were helping him arrange it!"

"So that's why Sassie and Marvin were spending so much time together! That's why they were having lunch at Eagle Ridge!" I said and thought, "So much for Polly's sources!" I couldn't wait to set her straight and quash that rumor!

"What about Brie?" I asked. "Did Marvin ever talk about her?"

"Brie?" Ken repeated, clearly surprised by my question.

"Well, when I was talking to one of the trainers yesterday after you left, he seemed to think that Marvin was responsible for Brie's new horse going lame. He said Brie thought the same thing."

"Really? That doesn't sound right," Ken said. "Marvin was an excellent vet, especially good with horses."

"And there's more. The word around the stables is that Brie is still upset about Marvin's breaking up with her even though that was well over a year ago now. Doesn't that seem a bit obsessive to you?" I asked.

"Yes, it does. And with her looks, she could have easily been dating other guys by now," Ken said.

I felt a twang of jealousy. So, Ken thought Brie was good looking. Humph! Well, she was, but that's beside the point. "Let it go," I told myself.

"Ken, Marvin was closer to you than to anyone. Do you have any idea who would have done this—cut his parachute rip cord, I mean?"

Ken paused. "No, I really don't. I thought about it all last night. Marvin never mentioned having a problem with anyone. I couldn't even think of anyone who would have benefited by Marvin's death. I suppose Tara would inherit his money, but frankly, I don't think there was all that much of it. And like I said, she loved him."

"Ken, did you know that Marvin had fired one of his employees recently?"

"Yes, he mentioned that he had to let an employee go. The fellow hadn't been with Marvin very long, maybe six months. But even so, it was hard for Marvin to fire him. I don't think he'd ever done that before."

"You're talking about Norman Trout, right?" I asked.

"I think that was the fellow's name. Why?"

"Did Marvin say why he had to fire Norman?"

Ken hesitated.

"Come on Ken, it can't hurt to tell me now," I urged him.

"Well, I suppose it can't. Marvin told me a few weeks ago that he'd found this new employee going through his files. Marvin walked in on him one night after the office was supposed to be closed. The guy tried to come up with some lame excuse but Marvin said he really didn't trust him after that. And so he fired him."

"What did Marvin think this guy was doing?" I pressed.

"He didn't know. That was the odd thing. Marvin said nothing was missing: no drugs, no files, and no money. But Marvin thought maybe he was looking up client names. And, you know, vets use some medicines that could be dangerous drugs," Ken said. "But the bottom line was, Marvin just didn't trust this guy anymore and he had to be able to trust the people he hired," Ken said.

"Yes, I can see that. And that makes more sense than what Harry Henry told me yesterday," I said.

"Who in the world is Harry Henry?" Ken asked.

"He's Brie's horse trainer. I met him at Galena Stables yesterday when I went to talk to Polly. Anyway, he said he and Brie were both convinced that Marvin had fired Norman Trout to blame him for Goldie's going lame."

"What nonsense!" Ken said. "First, Marvin was an excellent vet. Second, he was a stand up guy, and if he'd done anything wrong he would have taken the responsibility for it, not tried to blame someone else," Ken said. I expected steam to come through the phone any second now. I had never heard Ken so angry. "What do you know about this Harry Henry guy anyway?" Ken asked.

"I really don't know anything about him, other than what I just told you. He's Brie's horse trainer."

"Well, if he's disrespecting Marvin, I think Detective Cavanaugh ought to find out more about him," Ken said. "That's the first time I've ever heard someone talk like that about Marvin. And I don't believe a word of it."

"I think you're right. Maybe I can talk to Geri at the veterinary clinic this week. We've gotten to be friends over the years that I've been taking Truffs there. The receptionist always knows what's going on in a small office," I said. "And I'll ask a few discreet questions at the Antique Art Show this afternoon. Dara will be there, and she may have heard something about what happened. She's pretty well connected in town and not much happens that she doesn't know about" I said.

"Are you going to that?" Ken asked.

"Going? I'm doing the introductions and I'm on the panel!" I said.

"Oh, that's right. Sorry. I don't think I'm thinking straight. You did tell me about that, didn't you? I—I think I'm going to stay right here with Baxter."

Baxter was Ken's English Mastiff. He's a giant among giant dogs, weighing in at one hundred and eighty-five pounds. It took me awhile to get past his intimidating size but then I found he was really sweet. Truffs, however, still thinks otherwise.

"Of course," I said. "I don't expect you to want to socialize right now." I'd heard the pain in Ken's voice and I just wanted to give him a hug. There wasn't anything anyone could do to bring Marvin back but, more than ever, I wanted to make sure that whoever had done this didn't get away with it. "If there's anything I can do for you, please let me know."

"Thanks," Ken said. Then as if he was reading my mind, he said, "But don't go getting yourself involved in this. Leave it to our Sheriff's Department. Detective Cavanaugh will figure out who did this. Remember, someone really killed Marvin. This isn't a game. If you start snooping around, what's to stop that same person from going after you?" Ken asked.

"I'll be careful. I'll just talk to some friends. Galena's a small town. Someone here has to know what happened, or at least have a pretty good guess. And I'm going to find out," I said.

I looked down at my watch: 11:00 a.m. and I was still in my pajamas. "Yikes!" I thought. I was hoping to go for a run along the new Galena River Trail before this afternoon's event. There sure wouldn't be time to do that, get back here and clean up, and get to the Historical Society on time. Maybe I could get that run in afterward.

"Ken, I'm going to have to get going. The event starts at noon and I really should be there a little before that."

"No problem. I'll be here. Let me know how it goes," Ken said. I could hear Baxter give a mighty bark in the background.

"I will. And I'll be fine. I'm not going to do anything except maybe talk about what everyone else there is going to be talking about," I said. "And I'll let you know what I find out."

"All right," Ken said.

"Thanks for calling, Ken. We'll talk tonight," I said and hung up.

That left me thirty minutes to dress, check e-mail and make a phone call. I flicked on my computer and went to my closet. I selected white linen slacks, a blue and green hand-dyed silk top and sandals. I laid those out on the bed next to Truffs as my laptop went through its start-up chimes.

I turned on the shower and let it run. While the water was getting up to temperature, I clicked on my internet browser and went to Audible.com. I'd let my computer read me the New York Times' front page while I toweled off and dressed. Technology is so amazing these days. I suppose we are more amazed by technology developed in our lifetimes. I mean, cars are amazing, but I take them for granted. I'm sure younger generations take computers for granted. The funny thing is that we now get impatient with a computer taking minutes to do something that would have taken us hours to do without a computer.

Give it to us in minutes and we want it in seconds. Just human nature, I suppose.

As I flew back and forth between computer and bathroom I glanced longingly at the stairway leading up to my painting studio. Boy, I hated to miss a day of painting. And I'd be traveling this week to the Biltmore Summer Classic Horse Show! That meant more days out of the studio. I promised myself I'd at least sketch this evening and I'd take my traveling watercolor set with me to Asheville. That plan assuaged my longings a bit. So much for double tasking, I was triple tasking: dressing, listening to the news and planning my painting sessions. Maybe that's how those computer guys got the idea for windows. Sort of how the brain works, isn't it?

I did my quick version of makeup: moisturizer, mascara and lip gloss, then thought of being on stage and added eye shadow and liner. I blow-dried my hair and frowned as I ran my fingers through my too short locks. What had possessed me to have my hair cut this short? Oh well, it would grow out. I'd worn shoulder length hair since—since forever. But I'd had it cut to a two inch pixie cut this May. Spring fever must have gotten to me. Or maybe it was a reflection of the changes in my life. May was the last time I'd seen Mark. That was also when I'd met Ken. I refocused on my image in the mirror. O.K. I grabbed the hair gel and gooped a quarter size blob into the palm of my left hand, rubbed my hands together and ran my fingers through my hair just as my hairdresser had instructed me. It looked somewhat better.

Finishing touches applied to face and hair, I hopped into my clothes, patted Truffs and clicked off the computer. No time for e-mail. I'd catch up on that later.

Downstairs, I popped an English muffin into the toaster and called Tony and Louise. They were the folks who helped me maintain this country home. They tended the gardens, kept things around the house in working order, and watched Truffs when I traveled. We'd talked briefly about my trip to Asheville, but I wanted to make sure they had it on their calendar. Their phone rang without them picking up. Darn! Since it was Sunday, they were probably at church. I left a message reminding them that I'd be leaving Thursday morning and coming back Saturday. I knew they'd spend lots of time with Truffs while I was gone and that gave me great peace of mind.

I popped the last bite of muffin into my mouth and ran upstairs to grab my jogging clothes. If the event went until 4:00 p.m., I'd still have plenty of daylight time to get that run in on my way home. Nike's, socks, shorts and running top went into my brief case. I figured my old briefcase looked better than a gym bag and worked just as well. Besides, it made me smile to have jogging clothes in there instead of the deadly boring legal documents that I used to carry around.

I ran downstairs, grabbed two bottles of iced green tea from the fridge, and headed out the door. Halfway to Galena my cell phone rang. I fished the phone from my purse and was surprised to see Ken's number displayed. I clicked the answer button.

"Karen," Ken said. "There's something you should know. I just talked to Tara to see how she's doing. Detective Cavanaugh was there this morning and showed her a note they found in Marvin's pants pocket. It was a love letter and it wasn't from Tara," Ken said.

Chapter Six

Antique Art Show

I nearly drove off the road! "You're kidding! Does she know who sent it?" I asked.

"Brie Kellen sent it. And there's more. The letter said, 'If I can't have you then no one can.' Tara said that Brie had never stopped calling and writing to Marvin, even though he'd asked her to stop many times," Ken said.

"Wow! I suppose Detective Cavanaugh will be talking to Brie. I wonder if he'll arrest her based on this," I said.

"I don't know," Ken said. "I just wanted to tell you about it before you went to the art show and were talking to people. I'll let you go," Ken said and rang off.

I drove the rest of the way thinking about Marvin, Tara and Brie, and love gone wrong. Before I knew it, I was driving into town.

The Galena History Museum is on Bench Street overlooking downtown Galena. Bench Street, Galena's own "Great Street," is lined with beautiful brick mansions built in the mid 1800's. Back then, Galena was a veritable boom town. The Galena River was wide and deep enough to accommodate steamboats. Ships would come into Galena from the Mississippi River and take on loads of lead, zinc and supplies. After the Civil War, the nation's use of lead declined. And, as time went on, the Galena River silted in, preventing steamboats from stopping in Galena. The town endured a reversal of fortunes and Galena went into a hundred years sleep. In the 1970's, astute real estate developers bought downtown stores and Bench Street mansions for back taxes. They restored these downtown shops and homes to their former glory. Now, eighty-five percent of downtown Galena is on the National Historic Register. As a result of this grand scale renovation and the rediscovery of the natural beauty of this area, Galena has been enjoying a renaissance as a Midwestern tourist destination.

When I was doing research for my talk I came across some interesting history on the museum's building. The original Italianate mansion was built in 1858 by Daniel Barrows. The orange brick, three-story home was designed by William Dennison, the same architect who designed President Grant's home in Galena. In 1885, Barrows encountered financial difficulties and sold the house to John Ross. The house remained in the Ross family until Belle Ross died in 1922. Oddly enough, the house was then sold to the Odd Fellows who expanded the home and used it as their lodge until 1938. During the depression, the Odd Fellows had difficulty keeping up payments and the house went on the auction block. Luckily, the city of Galena was the successful bidder. City Hall moved into the first floor and the newly formed Historical Museum occupied the top two floors. Then, in 1967, City Hall moved to its current location on Main Street and the Historical Museum took over use of the entire building. Now there are 7,000 square feet of exhibition space, including an actual lead mine shaft.

I drove up to the Historical Society and, miracle of miracles, I found a parking spot right on Bench Street. I took that as a good omen for the Antique Art Show event. As I walked up the stairs to the front door, I mentally shifted gears. I couldn't wait to see what sort of paintings people brought us for identification.

Dara Brown must have spotted me as soon as I walked through the tall wood paneled front door. My eyes still hadn't adjusted to the dim interior light when I heard Dara's booming baritone call out my name. "Karen! Thank heavens you're here, dear. We're all upstairs. Bella's there too, setting up the buffet. I told them I knew you'd be here, never had a doubt in my mind!" she said. Apparently others hadn't been so sure. Jeez! The event wasn't set to start for half an hour, I thought. But before I could say anything, Dara was giving me a hug and leading me directly up the narrow, dark wood stairway.

Dara was the chairwoman and the major benefactor of the Galena Art Museum. Her family had made its fortune here, in the meat packing industry, generations ago. This spring, Dara and I had worked together on the Galena Art Museum's exhibition of Dutch floral paintings. Sharing a love of floral paintings and Galena's countryside, we'd quickly become friends.

Once we'd reached the second floor I could hear the buzz of activity in the large exhibition room to our left. But instead of heading up the few steps that would take us there, Dara turned to her right and motioned for me to join her in the room just down the hall where the topographical model of Jo Daviess County was exhibited. I looked at her quizzically but followed her lead.

"Something the matter?" I asked Dara when we'd both stopped in the far corner of the room, out of sight and earshot of the group getting ready for the upcoming event in the other room.

"I heard about Detective Cavanaugh's saying Marvin's parachute pull cord had been cut," Dara said, breathlessly. Tara called me last night. I spent the night at her place but I had to get back home early this morning. She shouldn't be alone. I think she's still in shock," Dara said.

"I imagine she is. It's so much to absorb! Does she have any idea who was responsible?" I asked.

"She told me that Brie had been writing to Marvin," Dara said in a whisper. "Can you imagine? It's been over a year since Marvin broke up with Brie, but she was apparently still obsessed with him!" Dara said.

"Do you think she's unstable enough to have killed Marvin?" I asked.

"Could be. Sort of hard to tell. She's such a loner that I don't think anyone really knows her," Dara said. "Brie left here when she was fifteen. She and her mother moved to New York so Brie could pursue a modeling career. She was fairly successful, from what I hear. Made a lot of money, but led a crazy life. She was in her mid twenties when she moved back here. Modeling careers are pretty short lived. I heard her mother stayed in New York. Brie had been in rehab to kick a drug habit. I think she came back here to start a normal life. Trouble was, she has no frame of reference for normal," Dara said.

"Well, that jibes with what Ken just told me." I filled Dara in on the ominous love letter.

"Oh, how awful!" Dara said. "I didn't realize she was so far out of control."

"You ride with her at Galena Stables don't you?" I asked.

"We both have our horses there, so we see each other occasionally. I don't compete anymore, so I don't really see that much of her even there," Dara said. "But enough about Brie. Let's talk about someone I like. How is Ken doing?" she asked.

"He's taking this all really hard," I said. "I want to make sure they find whoever's responsible, so, if you hear anything, please let me know, all right?"

"I'll keep my ears open for you. Let's talk at the end of the afternoon," Dara said conspiratorially. We looked each other in the eyes and nodded our silent agreement. "Come on," Dara said. "We'd better get in there."

We went back into the hallway and then up the few stairs that led to the largest of the exhibition spaces. This room was huge. It was added by the Odd Fellows to serve as their main lodge room. High on the south wall was Nast's "Peace in Union." I ignored the crowd in the room and walked directly to the painting. The work was all the more impressive in person. Its grey tones captured the somber mood of Lee's

43

surrender. The heroic scale of the work echoed the momentous nature of the occasion it depicted. Nast's skill as an artist comes through in the expressions of both the Generals and the observers around them.

"Imagine having that on your easel!" a man standing next to me said. Startled, I looked over to see Carl Castoni smiling at me. He had the most gorgeous dark brown eyes framed by thick curly lashes. Why isn't Brie focusing her attention on this guy, I thought.

"Carl, it's good to see you again. Are you involved with the Historical Society?" I asked. The Antique Art Show was co-sponsored by the Galena Art Museum and the Galena-JoDaviess County Historical Society. Since I'd never seen Carl at the Art Museum's events, I figured he must be involved with the Historical Society.

"Yes," he said. "Actually Marvin got me involved here when I joined his veterinary practice. He was a great supporter of the Society," Carl said, his tone much more sober now.

Hearing Marvin's name jolted me back to yesterday's tragic scene. I was at a momentary loss for words but finally stammered, "You must be really upset about losing him."

"I am," Carl said. "And I'd like to see whoever's responsible hung for it," he said through clenched teeth.

The abrupt change in his moods was disconcerting. The light had vanished from his eyes, replaced by a dark glare. I decided to take my chances and asked, "Carl, what do you know about Marvin's firing Norman Trout?"

"Who told you about that?" Carl asked sharply.

"I heard about it at the horse show yesterday," I said, evading a direct answer.

"Well, Norman was a strange character. Sort of hard to figure out what he was up to. He was new to town and said he'd always wanted to work with animals. We were short handed at the time and Marvin hired him. He didn't seem to know much about animals though. And, he seemed sort of afraid of horses. But basically he was

44

just running errands and doing odd jobs, and he seemed to want to stay, so Marvin kept him on," Carl said.

"So why did Marvin fire him, then?" I pressed.

"I guess there's no harm in telling you. Marvin found Norman going through client files one night when the clinic was supposed to be closed. That did it. Marvin fired him right then and there. We talked about it and never could figure out what Norman was up to, but we didn't think it could be good," Carl said.

"Did Norman ever threaten Marvin after Marvin fired him?" I asked.

"No, not that I ever heard about. Norman seemed to leave pretty quietly, actually."

"Carl, this may be sort of sensitive, but I really want to know. At the horse show yesterday, one of the trainers told me that Marvin had been responsible for Brie's new horse, Goldie, going lame. Is there any truth to that at all? I don't mean any disrespect to Marvin or to your practice. I'm just trying to get an idea of who could have had it in for Marvin."

Carl fumed for a minute, and then said, "Marvin was an excellent vet. I don't know who's spreading rumors like that, except maybe that blonde nutcase that was after him," Carl said.

"You mean Brie Kellen?" I asked. So much for my match-making thoughts about Brie and Carl.

"Ya, that's her name," Carl said. "She's a weird one. I wouldn't put it past her to have cut Marvin's parachute rip cord," Carl said.

I looked at him and I could tell he meant it. Was Brie really that nuts? Would she have had the strength to cut that cable? She did look like she was in excellent shape. Maybe she did do it.

Just then, a short, athletic looking man approached us. "Hello, he said. Sorry to interrupt you, I'm Roger Lesser, one of the event organizers. I need to go over the speaker arrangements with Karen."

"No problem," Carl said. "I'll talk to you later, Karen." Carl gave me a thousand dollar smile and nodded to Roger.

"Sure, I'll talk to you after the show," I responded.

Roger took my arm and ushered me to the elevated stage they had set up just to the right of "Peace in Union." "I want you to come and see how we've set up the microphone," Roger said. People will be streaming in here any minute for the lunch buffet, and then we'll start the show with your introduction.

"Fine," I said climbing up the three steps to the dais. There were four folding chairs set behind a long table draped with a white table cloth. Each chair had a small microphone on the table in front of it. To the left of the table stood a tall empty easel; to the right, the podium.

"I'll open the event with a welcome on behalf of the Historical Society and the Galena Art Museum and then I'll introduce you. You come up to the podium and give us some background information on our treasure there," Roger said, pointing to "Peace in Union." I'll act as emcee, so when you're finished, you can go back to the table. I'll go back to the podium and invite people from the audience to bring their art work directly up on stage and set it on the easel so the audience can see it. Here comes the rest of our panel now," Roger said.

Dara Brown and Lynne Shaw joined us on stage. "Lynne, you remember Karen from our last Art Museum board meeting, don't you?" Dara asked. Lynne was about my height, five-foot eight, with thick, long hair, parted in the middle and pulled up in a French twist. She wore a gorgeous turquoise squash blossom necklace and matching drop earrings.

"Of course," Lynne said, extending her hand to me. Lynne had joined the Galena Art Museum Board just last month. That's how we'd met and also how I knew that she lived in Galena and had a strong interest in Native American history in our area. I didn't know any more than that, but at the last board meeting Lynne had seemed bright, organized and energetic. I was looking forward to getting to know her better.

"So the plan is that I'll take the still-lifes, Roger will take the historical paintings, Dara will take the landscapes, and Lynne will take the portraits and any Native American influenced work that we might see, is that right?" I asked the others.

"That's right," Roger said. Lynne and Dara nodded their agreement.

"So, let the games begin!" I said, laughing. I really thought this would be fun.

"Well, actually, we'll open the doors at 1:00 p.m., but everyone will help themselves to the buffet table first, then they can eat lunch while they watch the festivities. Go help yourselves to plates now and you can bring them back up here," Roger said.

"We might as well enjoy lunch while we're doing this," Dara said.

"Good idea. Let's go see what Bella's prepared for us!" I responded and headed for the buffet with Lynne, Dara and Roger following me off the podium.

People began streaming into the room, some carrying framed paintings, some here for an interesting afternoon and to help support the Historical Society and the Art Museum.

Bella had created a gorgeous buffet. Large gold frames had been placed around the serving platters in keeping with the art theme. The centerpiece was a print of "View of Galena," an 1856 lithograph by E. Whitfield. The original work had been drawn from nature and depicts an overview of Galena, the river and its surrounding hills. The Historical Society sold these prints in their gift shop, so it would be good advertising for them and set the mood for the event at the same time. We circled the table and filled our plates with Bella's creations: fresh peaches marinated in port wine, Italian beef sandwiches, roasted vegetables and, for dessert, amaretti cookies. Steaming black coffee was served in a tall silver urn, the perfect complement to the sweetness of the almond cookies. As we finished circling the food table, Bella appeared with another tray heaped with the light buns filled with savory beef. "Bella!" What a feast you've prepared!" I said, as she placed the tray on the table. Bella was in her white coat and tall pleated chef's toque. This added a foot to her already substantial six-foot two inch frame.

"Karen!" Bella said, giving me a one-sided embrace as I held my plate out to the other side. Dara and Lynne had joined us now. I introduced Lynne to Bella. I knew Bella and Dara had met at my paddle boat event in May and had worked together on several events since then.

"Have you tried the peaches yet?" Bella asked. She kissed the tips of her fingers and said, "They're Georgia tree-ripened peaches. In another month or so you can try peaches fresh from my trees! You'll love them!"

"You can grow peaches up here?" Dara asked.

"You can! Starke Brothers' Reliance peaches. I have a huge crop this year! Bushels of them!" Nothing excited Bella like talking about food.

"I have to get the information on that. How long does it take for them to bear fruit?" Lynne asked.

"I'm told about five years," Bella said. "I was lucky enough to have them already at bearing age on my property when I bought my house here." One of Bella's young helpers dressed in white shirt and black pants approached our circle and whispered something in Bella's ear. "Excuse me," Bella said. "I'm needed in the kitchen."

"Of course," I said, and Bella was off following the young woman out the door as more folks streamed into the room.

As Dara, Lynne and I made our way back up to the dais, I noticed that the seats in the room were filling up. Roger joined us and, as we chatted over lunch, I learned that Roger owned a manufacturing company. He was also a horse enthusiast and so Dara, Lynne and

Roger all had that in common. They talked about their horses, and Galena Stables for a few minutes before the proceedings got underway.

At 1:30 p.m. precisely, Roger went to the microphone, welcomed everyone and introduced our little panel. Two hundred people had turned out and I saw at least a dozen of them had paintings on the chairs next to them. The room was packed and buzzed with anticipation. My brief speech went off smoothly and I sat down to a round of applause. Then we moved on to the main event!

Roger invited members of the audience to bring their paintings up to the easel. There was a moment of hushed silence as everyone looked around to see who would be first. Finally, an older gentleman stood and held a formal but primitive portrait.

"Come, bring that on up here," Roger said. "We'll have our panel take a look at it and place it on the easel here for the audience to see."

The older fellow made his way through the row of seats and I saw Bella come up from the back of the room and take the painting from him. Good idea, I thought. We should have had runners to carry the paintings for folks, like we do at the Galena Art Museum's annual art auction. But this will work.

Bella carried the painting up on stage and placed it on the table for our inspection. Lynne was our portrait point person, so she'd give the commentary, but we all leaned in to take a good close look at the work. Lynne pulled out a magnifying glass from her shoulder bag and looked for a signature. "This had to be by Sheldon Peck," Lynne whispered to us. "I know this artist's work. The Whitney Museum in New York showed a number of his works at the Bicentennial Exhibition. He didn't sign his paintings but I know his style. He traveled through here in the 1860's. We couldn't have a better start!"

Lynne stood and placed the painting on the easel. She faced the audience and said, "This is an oil painting, about twenty inches by sixteen inches. You'll notice the frame is actually painted on the canvas in a technique called *trompe l'oeil*, in which the artist simulated wood grain. Can you tell us your name and how you acquired this painting?" Lynne asked the gentleman who'd brought it. She elicited the history of the painting, what art dealers call the provenance of the piece, from the gentleman.

The gentleman's name was Arthur Westwood and the painting was a portrait of his great uncle, Ralph Westwood. Ralph had been a prominent physician in Galena during Galena's boom-time. Arthur had inherited the painting and that was all that he knew about the work.

Lynne thanked Arthur and said, "This painting was done by a well known traveling portrait artist, named Sheldon Peck. Sheldon Peck lived in Lombard, Illinois. He was a farmer and during the off season he traveled and accepted commissions for portraits. A pair recently sold for $65,000 and Peck charged $50 for a double portrait.

There's an inscription on the back of the canvas that reads: "Presented to Dr. Ralph Westwood, Galena, Illinois, by the grateful family of Miss Marjorie May Girot, 1860." Perhaps Dr. Westwood saved this young woman's life, and her family commissioned this portrait as a thank you. In the 1800's, portrait artists traveled to major cities and painted portraits while they were there. They lined up commissions before their arrival, through ads in the local newspapers. Peck's style of painting was simple and direct. Some might call this style primitive, but it is highly collectible. I'd estimate the value of this painting at $30,000, though I am sure it's a priceless family heirloom to you and your children," Lynne concluded.

"It will stay in our family, that's for sure," Arthur said with pride. "Thank you." Arthur sat down to a hearty round of applause and Bella retrieved the painting from the easel and returned it to him.

That seemed to break the ice. There was a steady flow of people with paintings: Mrs. Roundtree with a watercolor landscape, a young woman with a civil war era battle scene painting, an unsigned still life of fruits and flowers, another portrait, a quite valuable painting of Blackhawk, and then I saw it.

A young woman in her twenties presented a painting of two white magnolia blossoms on a deep blue velvet draped cloth. My heart pounded. This had to be a copy. I held my breath as Bella placed the painting on the table in front of me. I had seen a very similar painting at the Art Institute in Chicago. This couldn't be by the same artist, could it? "Can I borrow your magnifying glass, Lynne?" I asked, as calmly as I could.

"Sure," she said and passed the silver handled magnifier to me.

I held the glass over the lower right hand of the painting and gasped. There it was! "Martin Johnson Heade" painted in the distinctive red lettering he used for his signatures. But could this be an imitation? Dara gave me a quizzical look and leaned in next to me. "What?" she asked in a whisper. I guess my excitement was obvious. Even though I tried to remain calm, my hand was shaking as I moved the magnifying glass over the rest of the painting. It was all there. Everything was consistent with this being done by the hand of a master: the exquisite brush strokes, the minute color changes, the deft handling of the shadows, the texture of the petals!

I knew Dara was familiar with Heade's work from the May exhibition at the GAM that had featured American floral paintings. I knew she'd recognize his name even if she hadn't yet recognized this as his work. I held the magnifying glass over the signature and said, "Dara, take a look at this." She leaned over the painting and squinted into the magnifying glass. Dara let out a whistle and looked at me.

"Do you think this is real?" she asked me, sotto voce.

I looked at her and nodded slowly. "I do," I said. "I really do!"

Dara reached over and grabbed my arm! Lynne looked at us both and got out of her chair and leaned over my shoulder to take a better look at the painting. "Whose work do you think this is?" she whispered to me.

"Martin Johnson Heade. Ameican, circa 1880," I said.

"Heade! Really? A real Heade?" she exclaimed.

By now it was obvious to Roger and the audience that something unusual was going on up here. The buzz in the room escalated as everyone whispered to their neighbor.

I rose from the table and lifted the painting very, very carefully! Feet don't fail me now! I placed the painting on the easel and smiled at the audience. "Could you tell us your name and how you acquired this work?" I asked the young woman, who clearly didn't have a clue about the value of her painting. If she did, she wouldn't be walking around with it so casually.

"My name is Liz Seelig. The painting's been in my family for years. I remember my grandmother having it in her dining room. She was an artist and rather liked this work."

I'll bet she did, I thought. "And did she live in this area?" I asked.

"No. My family is from upper New York, the Catskill area. I moved here with my husband when I got married. Mom gave this to me as a wedding present, and to remember my grandmother by, too, I think. She said Grandma would have liked me to have it. Sort of an old painting, but I like it too, because it was hers," she said.

"Well, I have an idea you'll want to take very good care of this family heirloom. It's also a national treasure. This is an original still life painting by Martin Johnson Heade. The last Heade to come on the market sold for 1.2 million dollars."

Pandemonium broke out in the room! People applauded, hooted and howled. Liz collapsed into her chair. She looked up at me and our eyes met. Liz got up, walked up to the edge of the table and I leaned over toward her. "Are you sure?" she asked. I could barely hear her above the crowd. Roger, Dara and Lynne were now all standing up around the easel looking at the painting.

"Well, I am pretty sure, yes. It's very clearly signed; and the quality of the work, the style, the subject, the location where the painting was acquired all fits. Heade lived in the Catskill area and took trips to St. Augustine, Florida where he probably painted this magnolia.

He did a series of those gorgeous southern magnolias. You'll want to have this painting properly appraised by an art dealer, and you'll want to have it insured. I'd do that right away if I were you," I said.

"Thank you. Thank you very much," Liz stammered. I think she was going into some sort of shock.

"Would you like some help with this painting, Liz?" I asked her?

"I'll help her," Bella piped up, appearing next to the young woman. I think you'll need some help making it through this crowd with that!"

Everyone was rushing from their seats now, jockeying for a closer look at the painting. It had been sitting there all along. Funny what a price tag will do, I thought.

Roger tapped on the microphone. "Folks! Folks! Let's form a line here, if you'd like to come take a look at the painting. I'd say we've had a success here at the Antique Art Show! Come on up here and stand by your painting, Liz," Roger said.

Bella, Dara, Lynne, Roger and I formed a flanked guard around Liz and her Heade as folks rushed forward to see the million dollar painting. After a quick look, people left to spread the word of Galena's newest hidden treasure.

Chapter Seven

Galena River Trail

As Lynne and I left the Historical Society's main gallery she asked, "So, what do you plan to do with the rest of the day? It'll be sort of hard to top discovering an original Heade painting!"

I laughed. "Yes, I suppose it will be. I was just going to go for a jog on the new River Trail. I haven't been on it yet, have you?" I asked as we walked down the dark wood stairway to the first floor.

"Yes, I have. I love it. I live right across the street from it so it's become my favorite jogging trail."

"Really! I have my jogging clothes in here," I said, lifting the brief case in my right hand. I was just going to make a quick change in the ladies room and head over there."

"That sounds great! After Bella's lunch, I could use a bit of a workout!" Lynne said.

"Well, why don't you come with me? We could jog together, if you don't mind waiting for me for a minute while I change here," I said.

"No, that sounds great. But you don't have to change here. Come on over to my place and we can both change there and walk over together," Lynne said. "I'm walking home, so I can meet you at my place. It's the miners' cottage on Park Avenue, on the south side of the river, right by the underpass to the trail."

"Great. In fact, I can drive you home if you'd like. I'm parked right outside," I said.

We popped into the Boxster and took Bench Street back to Highway 20, turned left on the bridge and then took the first left to Park Street and Lynne's home. Miners' cottages are a Galena classic. Built by the poor mining families of the mid 1800's, they are small, often made of local limestone. And Lynne's fit the bill perfectly.

I parked in front and climbed out. The stone steps to the front door were worn with age. The doorway was low and I could just walk in without ducking. Lynne had decorated her home in period colors and antiques. The place had a cozy, comfortable feeling.

"I know it's small, but it's perfect for me. It's close to town so I can walk to all the weekend events. And I travel most of the week for work so I'm glad to have neighbors close by," Lynne said.

"What do you do?" I asked.

"I'm in pharmaceutical sales. I sell to hospitals and doctors' offices in the tri-state corner," Lynne said.

I glanced at the paintings on Lynne's living room wall and was drawn to a portrait of an Indian in full native dress. I looked at the signature and read, "George Catlin." Good heavens! Apparently selling pharmaceuticals was very lucrative.

Are you familiar with Catlin's work?" Lynne asked.

"Well, I've seen it in museums out west. It's spectacular," I replied.

"Thanks," Lynne said. "If you're interested in Native American artifacts, take a look in here. It's sort of a hobby of mine," Lynne said as she walked over to a long display case standing against the living room wall. I joined her and looked through the glass door of the case. Lynne flipped the switch on the side of the cabinet and lights illuminated the contents.

"That's Pueblo black pottery, isn't it?" I'd seen one at the Santa Fe Museum and I knew they sold for several hundred thousand dollars if they were in original, good condition. And this was in beautiful condition.

"Yes, I was lucky enough to purchase it on a trip to New Mexico thirty years ago. It was a cross-country driving trip. I found this in a little shop along the way and bought it for a few hundred dollars. That was a lot to me at the time and of course I had no idea it would become such a collector's item. That trip sparked my interest in Native American artifacts. I lived out west for the first twenty years of my career. I moved here five years ago to head-up our regional sales. Selling my place in California gave me enough liquidity to buy that painting you were admiring. Besides the difference in cost of living, the best part of moving here was discovering the Native American history in this area. I can't believe how little documentation there is about the Midwest's Native American population. I'm starting my own collection, things I pick up at auctions. But something just as interesting, that I actually find on hikes, are these flutes, scrapers and arrowheads," Lynne said, pointing at the middle shelf full of triangular shaped stones.

"Where do you find these?" I asked.

"I bought a tract of land in the country. I lease the grazing rights to a local farmer, but I hike on it a lot. All those scarpers you see there I found on my hikes. Most of them were just laying in the streambed. This is an arrowhead I found there, too," Lynne said, pointing to a light grey triangular shaped stone. See all the chipping along the edges? That shows it was hand made, not a naturally occurring bit of rock," Lynne said.

"Wow!" I had no idea you could just find these things laying around. I've found fossils on my property, but I haven't found Indian artifacts," I said.

"Maybe you will," Lynne said, "now that you know what you're looking for. If you have a spring starting on your property, there's a good chance you'll find scrapers there and maybe even arrowheads. Think about it. People need water and going to the source of the water at the spring site would be the cleanest water. And downstream would be a natural place to clean the hides and that sort of thing."

"I've heard about the Fox and the Sauk Indians who lived here. Do you think these were made by them?" I asked.

"No, I think these predate the Fox by about 1,000 years!"

"What!" I exclaimed.

"Really! These are from the late Woodland Period of the North American Indian artifacts, probably around 800 AD."

"I had no idea! You'll have to come on a hike with me on my property sometime. It would be fascinating to see what we find," I said.

"I'd enjoy that," Lynne said. "Well, we'd better get going if we're going to get that run in. You can change in the bathroom," Lynne said. "I'll go get ready myself. My bedroom's upstairs, so I'll be back in a few minutes. The bath is right through there," Lynne said, pointing to the adjoining kitchen. "It looks like it was added to the house by a former owner. This cottage was probably built with an outhouse out back," Lynne said and then headed up the narrow stairs along the far wall.

Ten minutes later, we were in our jogging clothes, doing stretches in Lynne's front yard. Lynne looked at me and said, "I talked with Sassie Ballantine this morning."

"How is she doing? And how is Captain Ed?" I asked.

"Sassie said that Detective Cavanaugh had been at their place for over an hour yesterday. He wanted to know every detail about the balloon ride: who'd been on the ground crew, who'd driven the truck, where they'd taken off, just everything. She said he had a million questions for them."

"Does Captain Ed or Sassie have any idea who could have cut that pull cord?" I asked.

"They have no idea." Lynne shook her head. "It's so awful," she said, her voice trailing off.

"I know. I know," I said. We stretched in silence for a few more minutes, lost in our own thoughts about Marvin.

"Are you ready?" I asked.

"I'm ready," Lynne said. We headed out at an easy pace across Park Street and down the grass hillside leading to the park. We jogged under the bridge, through the parking lot and made our way to the start of the trail.

"So you've never been here before?" Lynne asked.

"No, this is my first time on the trail," I said.

"Well, it's a great jogging trail. Really level, and there's a marker every half mile. How far do you want to go?" Lynne asked.

"A five-mile jog would be perfect for me. How about you?" I asked.

"I usually only do three myself. How about we compromise? There's a rest area two miles out. How about if we turn around there?" Lynne suggested.

"Sure," I said. It would be an interesting diversion to have a jogging partner and it would give me a chance to get to know Lynne a little better.

The trail started as a paved surface and in a minute or so we were at another underpass.

"That's the Canadian National Railroad track above us," Lynne said.

As we came out of the underpass a sign caught my eye. "Hey, look at that," I said, nodding to the right. A park sign said "Natural Spring" with an arrow pointing off the trail to our left. "Want to go take a look?" I asked.

"Sure," Lynne said agreeably. She'd probably already checked it out but I love natural springs and I didn't want to take a chance on forgetting to stop on the way back. We slowed our pace to a walk and followed the side trail towards the woods. In about a tenth of a mile the trail ended at a little pond. I looked around and was surprised not to see the water running out from the base of a hill into a stream like the natural springs on my property. This was a quiet shallow pool of clear water, about thirty feet long and maybe ten feet across.

We both stooped down at the edge of the pond. "Look," Lynne said pointing into the water about a foot from the pond's edge. I stared at the water and saw air bubbles form at the bottom of the pond and float the few inches to the surface. A moment later I saw another and then another.

"Huh! The water's bubbling up right from the ground!" I said.

"Yup. It's an Artesian Spring," Lynne said.

A frog jumped at the edge of the pond, startling us both. We gasped and then laughed. "All right. Back to our workout," Lynne said, rising and heading back to the main trail.

"That was fun!" I said. We jogged in companionable silence on the level, empty trail. In a few minutes the sounds of traffic faded behind us and we were surrounded by trees on both sides of us. The city seemed miles away.

"How did the City get the land for this trail?" I asked.

"They joined forces with the Illinois Department of Natural Resources to buy the old railroad right-of-way. This trail was created on the old spur track bed. The spur ran three and a half miles from Galena to the Burlington Railroad line that runs along the Mississippi River. The spur was put in around 1886 and carried passengers until 1940. After that it was used just for freight until about 1960. Then it was pretty much abandoned until this trail opened a few years ago," Lynne said between deep jogging breaths.

"You're quite a historian," I said smiling at Lynne.

"I like history," Lynne said.

A cloud of sulfur butterflies rose up from the trail as we jogged. We passed an old building on our right at the half mile marker and then a farm to our left. There was a sign warning that vehicles shared the trail for the next mile. I looked around and it was hard to imagine where the cars would come from. I guessed just from the farm that we had passed on our left.

After a mile, there were barricades in the trail that stopped cars from going any further along the trail. As we got into our jogging pace conversation dropped away. Tree branches formed a leafy arch over the trail. Light filtered through the trees. The temperature was cooler here along the shadowed trail.

At the one and a half mile marker there was a gorgeous limestone outcropping in the woods to our left. Then the trail took a big sweeping bend to the right.

"There it is!" I said between huffing breaths.

"What?" Lynne asked.

"The river! I had always thought this trail would run parallel to the Galena River," I said.

"Well, it sort of does," Lynne said. "But the river jogs around and there's enough woods in between that you only see the river a few times along the trail. Whew! Our turn around is just up there," Lynne said, panting.

In a minute, the two-mile marker came into view. There was a picnic table situated on a small grassy area to the right of the trail overlooking the river. "What a gorgeous view!" I said. The river was substantially wider and looked much deeper here than in Galena. We were standing at the top of a bluff overlooking the river about thirty feel below us. The far shore was almost level with the river. There was an old dock there.

"That's the old brewery building," Lynne said. An abandoned two-story, red-brick building stood on the opposite shore. The windows had long since been broken or removed. The roof had holes in several places.

"Looks like that place hasn't been used in eons," I said. As we stood looking down at the river a kayak came into view. There were two men in the kayak with several boxes balanced between them. "That's odd. Think they're camping?" I asked.

"With their gear in boxes?" Lynne replied. "You'd think maybe a backpack or a rucksack would make more sense for camping."

"Well, a kayak sure is a funny way to move stuff. And what's out here anyway? I haven't seen any buildings except that abandoned brewery," I said.

"There are a few," Lynne said. "Roger has his telephone factory somewhere out here, I think."

"Roger? Roger who?" I asked.

"Roger Lesser. The fellow on our panel today," Lynne said.

"Oh, right. So, his company makes telephones?" I asked.

"I hear they make the hand-sets and other parts for telephones. I think that's his main business. Must be how he funds his horse riding."

"Hey, look," I said, pointing down at the kayakers. They seemed to be slowing. The fellow at the rear put his paddle into the water and steered the kayak in toward the far shore.

"Yeah," Lynne whispered. The kayakers had now stopped. One of the fellows threw a line around the post of the old dock. We watched in silence as the forward fellow in the kayak climbed onto the rickety dock.

Once he was up there, he lay down on the dock and reached down. The fellow still in the kayak grabbed the boxes and handed them up to him in turn. Lynne and I looked at each other. What was this? Silently, we both crouched down so we could watch without being seen by the kayakers.

The fellow on shore carried both boxes into the abandoned building He reemerged about five minutes later and climbed back into the kayak. Then they were off, silently moving back up the river from the direction they'd appeared. Soon they were around the river bend and out of our line of sight.

"That was really weird," I said.

"Yeah, it was," Lynne said. "What do you think we just saw?"

"I have no idea!" I said. "And why would you leave something in an old building? And why go through the trouble to carry it by kayak?" I asked.

"I wonder if there's a road that leads to that old brewery," Lynne said.

"Well there must be. How would they have gotten supplies otherwise?" I said.

"Could have had everything moved in and out by rail. Remember, we're standing on an old railroad bed. Maybe they just unloaded supplies right here from the railroad and then moved the stuff across the river by boat."

"Well, then how did the workers get there?" I asked.

"Good point. I guess there must be a road," Lynne said. Then, looking at her watch she asked, "Ready to head back?"

"Yup. Let's go," I said.

The jog back was as gorgeous and peaceful as the trip out. We saw only one other person on the trail, a bicyclist, the whole way back.

As we jogged through the Canadian National Railroad underpass the sounds of Highway 20 traffic drifted down to us.

We stopped for a moment at the end of the trail, stretched our legs, and then walked back up the hill to Lynne's place. I didn't want to change into my good clothes, so I just put them and my briefcase in the Boxster's front trunk and headed back home. It had been quite a day. A real Heade! I couldn't get over it!

Chapter Eight

The Orchid Painting

I walked into the kitchen from the garage and found Truffs waiting for me, as usual. I scooped her up in my arms and stroked her long, silky fur. "I'll bet you're ready for dinner," I said, rubbing her jet black head. She blinked her green eyes in agreement.

I placed Truffs on the red brick kitchen floor and she led the way to the pantry, her full black tail held high. Something on the counter next to the sink caught my eye. Tony and Louise had left a gorgeous daylily bouquet on the counter for me. I was sure it was from them. They tend my gardens and they had planted hundreds of lilies in the rock garden. There were yellow, orange and red daylilies; pink and white Asian lilies; and the always glorious white Madonna lilies. They were at their peak right now. Each intensely colored blossom lasted only a day but the bouquet lasted a week as new flowers opened. Each green bud would quadruple in size and open into a brilliant, colorful lily. How they did this after they were picked was a mystery. But they did. Miracles were all around us if we were open to seeing them. These flowers would be gorgeous in a painting, I thought. Truffs had taken her position in front of her kitty buffet area. Her eyes followed me as I selected a can of Fancy Feast for her from the pantry and placed the minced contents on a pale blue plate hand painted with a grey mouse in the center.

I'd had a set of six plates made by a local potter last year as Truffles' birthday present. O.K., so maybe I do spoil her. But her loving presence is so much a part of my life that I like to indulge her. And the plates do make me smile.

Each plate features a mouse in a different activity: running around the edge of the plate, peaking over the side, sleeping with its feet tucked under its tiny head, looking over its shoulder, and holding a tiny piece of cheese. I found them entertaining and I liked to think that Truffles did too.

Once Truffs was fed, I went to the phone to call Ken. The red light on my machine was blinking and I played back a message from Marshall Ottilier. Marshall, the owner of the New York gallery that shows my work, was looking for a shipping date for the orchid painting I'd promised him. The painting was nearly finished. Another day in the studio would do it and I promised myself that day would be tomorrow. I'd return Marshall's call tomorrow when I could tell him the painting was completed and drying!

I dialed Ken's number and he picked up on the third ring. I filled him in on the surprising events at the Historical Society but, in his depressed state, he wasn't going to get excited about anything except Marvin's killer being found. Ken didn't want to talk long, but he did say he'd pick me up for the winery event at 6:00 p.m. tomorrow. I took that as a good sign.

I tucked in early with Truffs nestled between my ankles. When morning came I woke to find she'd made her way to my pillow, nestled against the top of my head. I reached up and petted her. She responded by licking my hand with her raspy tongue. "Morning to you too!" I said.

We made our way down to the kitchen where I had strong black coffee and Truffs had her usual morning can of Fancy Feast Ocean Fish. I don't know how she could eat anything that smelled like that, especially at 6:00 a.m. But, then again, I knew only too well that she'd eat a mouse, given half a chance.

I was surprised to hear the phone ring while I was still sipping my first cup of coffee on the screened-in porch. Caller ID's mechanical voice announced: "Da-ra Bro-wn." Dara? I looked at my watch. It wasn't even 6:30 a.m. I cold shiver ran down my spine as I went to the phone. This was way too early for good news.

"Good morning, Dara," I said.

"Morning, Karen. But I'm not sure about good. Are you sitting down?" Dara asked.

"No."

"Well, I think you'd better," Dara said.

"What? What happened?" I asked.

"All right. I just heard this. Detective Cavanaugh's been called out to Galena Stables. They just found Brie's body!"

"What! Who found her—her body? You mean she's dead! What happened?"

"Whoa! Slow down. I don't have all of the details. I just know that Harry called the Sheriff's Department ten minutes ago. The Sheriff's Department called Adam Hall, the manager of Galena Stables," Dara said.

"That happened ten minutes ago and you already know about it?"

"Honey, my roots run deep in this old grapevine. But don't worry about how I know. I have it right. And yesterday you said you wanted to stay up on what was happening with the investigation, so I figured you'd want to hear this," Dara said.

"Well, I do. I want to hear whatever you find out. Thanks! Did you hear what happened to her? I mean, how she died?"

"I heard that it looks like a drug overdose. They'll do an autopsy to be sure but that's what I'm hearing now."

"A drug overdose? I thought she came here to get away from drugs," I said.

"Well, I guess she didn't. That's really a shame. Such a beautiful girl and so young," Dara said.

"Yes, she had her whole life ahead of her. Well, let me know if you hear anything else. Thanks for calling me," I said.

"No problem. Sorry to start your day this way," Dara said.

"Me too. But better to know. Do you think the two deaths are related somehow?" I asked.

"You mean Marvin and Brie?" Dara asked. "I hadn't thought so. But I suppose she could have been so upset about Marvin that she went back to drugs. Maybe she took too much by mistake or maybe it was just bad drugs."

"I suppose it could be," I said. "Or Brie could have killed Marvin and then taken an overdose of drugs out of guilt," I hypothesized.

"Hmm, she was a bit strange, but she seemed like she loved Marvin. I don't think she'd have killed him or anyone else," Dara said.

"Just thinking of the possibilities," I said. "I'm not saying I think she did kill Marvin. If there's any connection, I'd say she was grief stricken and went back to drugs to try to escape her grief," I said.

"Well, I'll let you know what else I hear. I'll keep my ear to the ground," Dara said.

"Thanks again, Dara," I said and we hung up.

Brie dead! How horrible. I shook my head and walked back upstairs to dress. It was too early to call Ken right now. I'd do that in a bit. There wasn't anything he could do so why take a chance on waking him up with this sort of news. I thought of rushing out to the stable, but what good would that do? I'd see the horse folks at the winery event tonight and I could talk to them then. I had promised myself I'd finish that painting this morning and that's what I'd do. But before I could paint I needed to relax and nothing works better than a good workout. Well, almost nothing.

Since I'd done my four miles yesterday afternoon, I figured I could get by with just my Body Electric floor exercises today. I popped in a video by Margaret Richards, my exercise guru, and worked my abs, glutes, deltoids and biceps.

That done, I had breakfast on the patio, followed by a quick shower. I changed into blue jeans and white tee shirt, then called Ken and gave him the news about Brie. Ken was quiet for a minute, then he said, "Two deaths so close together. What is going on here?" I heard both anger and anguish in his voice. There wasn't much I could say except to assure him we'd get to the truth behind both Brie and Marvin's deaths. When we hung up, I took a walk through the gardens to clear my head and then headed up the circular stairs to my studio.

The prior owner of my house had the unusual hobby of collecting and preserving silos. The stairs to my third floor studio were located in a silo that he had moved and attached to this house. Going around and around I ascended the metal stairs and let the everyday world drop away.

I walked into the long, high-ceilinged studio and smiled at the light flowing in through the wall of twelve-foot high, north facing windows. The studio was painted a dark greenish-gray to prevent natural light from bouncing off the walls. I strove to create an atmosphere of peaceful beauty in my studio and in my paintings. I turned on the CD player and Jean Pierre Rampal's ethereal flute music floated through the air.

My model, a cream colored pansy orchid with velvety crimson markings, stood on a wooden pedestal to the left of my easel. I preferred painting my orchids with light flowing from the upper left. This was consistent with most viewers' natural tendency to read paintings from left to right.

I took my seat in front of my easel and examined the nearly completed painting. Studying a painting in progress with "fresh eyes" before starting to paint was a long standing artistic aide. It helped me see clearly what needed to be done next. I took in the graceful arc of the twin flowering stems. The pansy orchid had a joyful feel to it. The lower petal of each blossom resembles a lady's colorful skirt, the two petals above that, her outstretched arms, the top petals her hat and winged collar. Seven of these flowers graced each of the arching stems and danced in the falling light. A fan of narrow pointed orchid leaves spread out behind the blossoms. This pansy orchid was indeed a special treasure of an orchid. It was harder to grow than the phalaenopsis orchids that populated most of my window sills. Pansy orchids bloom only once a year and the flowers are not as long lived as the moth orchid, the common name for the phalaenopsis orchid due to its large wing-like petals. Still, this little beauty held a special place in my heart and I couldn't wait to paint those final strokes that would preserve it in the painting.

Getting down to business, I arranged my palette on a table to my right and my brushes, in order of size, on a separate table to my left. I squeezed fresh paint from metal tubes and arranged small piles of pigment along the edge of my palette. With my palette knife, I worked each pile of color into a buttery smooth state which would be receptive to the tip of my brush. This was a lot of preparation, but it set the stage so that the painting would flow smoothly from eye, to mind, to canvas. Or was that mind, to eye, to canvas? Possibly the latter, but that is a philosophical discussion for another time.

A successful painting is more than a technical collection of brush strokes. It starts with an inspiration—the conveyance of the artist's concept at the core of the work. Here, the concept was the movement of light from above, falling across the blooms. Light piercing darkness, revealing beauty. Maybe that was the essence of hope. Someone once said that my work was about transformation. That may be so. Here, light transforms the darkness, illuminating the beauty of the blossoms.

There is a long history of symbolism in still-life painting. I like to use those symbols to add another layer of meaning to my work. For instance, this painting includes an antique gold timepiece on the table next to the orchid. The watch symbolizes the fleeting nature of time and life itself. The painting seems to say: "Look, see the beauty and dance like this orchid while you can!"

Finally, I was ready to paint. I picked up dark, rich green paint with the tip of my brush and followed the twists and turns of the leaf with my eyes as I created its image on my painting panel. This was the dark green shadow color. Next, I picked up a bit of yellow green and moved my brush along the path of light on the leaf's edge in the painting. The leaf sparked to life.

Each stroke was an observation: the leaf curves here, the light peaks there. The totality of these observations formed the image on the painting panel. An artist learns to communicate in the language of paint.

An artist's tools to create a realistic painting are: drawing, value (light and dark), color, edges (soft and hard), and paint quality (thick or thin). I checked each of these in my work and made a few adjustments where it was necessary to refine the form or to create a sense of light on the canvas. The movement of light, reinforced by the design of the composition, was what would lead the viewer's eye through the painting. I wanted to share the delight I felt on seeing the light fall on the beautiful form of the orchid flower, the transparent shadows, the curve of the petals, and the glisten of a dew drop. I would translate all this into paint for the viewer to experience with me.

It takes many hours of painting in order to capture a moment in time. But, to have a worthy painting, it should be not just any moment that is captured. It needs to be the moment when the artist is truly seeing and feeling the beauty of nature. Maintaining that vision of light and beauty, that connection to something eternal, while painting, and somehow putting that into the painting—that is what makes a truly transcendent painting. The architect, Mies van der Rohe, said, "God is in the details." That seems to be the case with paintings as well. Spending an extra day or two on a "completed" painting, allows me to bring that work to another level. The subtle adjustments of light and shadow, the addition of a drop of water, a hovering butterfly, all of these small additions are there for the viewer to see so they will continue to find delight in the work each time they view it. And for me, there is the joy of staying in that frame of mind, of continuing to see the beauty.

The hours between 8:00 a.m. and 5:00 p.m. flew by in a minute. I stopped only once, at noon, to rest my eyes and have a quick lunch. Now I sat back and studied my work. Done! I jotted some notations in my sketchbook and looked at my watch.

5:30 p.m.! Oh, I hated to leave! But Ken would be here in an hour! I cleaned my brushes, placed my palette in my refrigerator, (yes, I keep my palette refrigerated when I'm not painting), returned my orchid to its home by the window, and closed the studio door behind me.

That left me fifteen minutes for an insto-presto change. I opened my closet doors and looked at the row of hanging garments. What to wear to a winery tour? My pale yellow linen slacks and jacket were an option. Then there was the long, sleeveless, maroon Armani dress. Hmm... Chardonnay or Bordeaux? I went for the Bordeaux. Looking in the mirror, I added the matching woven belt that fell around my hips. The belt reminded me of the giant beads hanging from the nuns' waists when I was in grade school. I zipped up the side-zipper, mentally thanking Giorgio for not using the impossible-to-dress-alone back zipper. That little adjustment brought the dress into fairly close contact with most of my torso. Walking in this number was made possible by two ample side slits running from ankle to thigh. This certainly didn't remind me of a nun's habit anymore.

I slipped into strappy Cole Haan sandals and hoped we wouldn't actually be walking among the grape vines. Dinner on the patio and a sampling of the local vintner's efforts were more what I had in mind. And since Polly had coordinated this with Clay, I figured it would be more of a sipping and dining than a stomping and tromping expedition. And so it proved to be.

Chapter Nine

The Winery

Ken picked me up in his silver truck and held the passenger door open for me. It took some serious skirt-hiking to make the giant step up into the seat, but I managed it, much to Ken's bemusement. Ken was in well-fitting blue jeans, a crisply pressed white shirt and loafers. He looked great. Ken was sensitive, intelligent and enjoyed life. Most of the fellows I'd dated in the past, including Mark, had been strong in the intelligent department and low in the sensitivity and enjoying life departments. I was finding sensitivity an attractive quality these days.

We rode in silence for a few minutes, the shadow of the last two days hanging over us. "Are you ready to go to a party after all that's happened?" I asked.

"I'll admit I'm not in a party mood. But I want to hear what people say about who they think killed Marvin. And now, with Brie, well, I want to hear what people are saying about that too," Ken said.

"That's a good idea. Maybe there's more of a connection between Marvin and Brie than we know about. Maybe we'll be able to learn something about that as well," I said.

"I suppose that the odds are that the same person was responsible for both of their deaths," Ken said soberly.

"Yes, I think so. Do you know what Marvin and Brie had in common, besides the fact that they dated a few years ago?" I asked.

"Horses," Ken replied quickly.

"O.K. And what about people? Who were the people they interacted with?" I said, shifting into Nancy Drew mode.

"What about that groom? What's his name? The fellow who worked for Brie," Ken said.

"You mean Norman Trout," I said. "Yes, both Marvin and Brie had employed him."

"That is sort of a strange coincidence, don't you think?" Ken said.

We turned off Blackjack Road, and followed the two-mile long Sawmill Road up, down and around to Highway 84. We rode by the new River Ridge School and took a right onto the two lane Highway 20. Highway 20 was a steady mix of trucks, tourists and weekend commuters. I knew because I'd been one of those commuters for a while, before I left my law practice to live in nature's wonderland. A Galena by-pass is in the works, as well as plans for turning this twisty, two-lane road into a modern four lane freeway. Even though the project is long past due, it will probably still take another ten years.

We took a left off of Highway 20 onto Scales Mound Road just before the town of Elizabeth. Scales Mound Road rides the hilltop ridges and offers spectacular views of the undulating countryside. The rows of soybean and corn defined the contours of the hills and valleys.

"Gorgeous out here," I said.

"Yes it is," Ken said looking at me. "And so are you."

I blushed the color of my dress and smiled at him. "Thanks," was all I managed to say. I was really getting to like this fellow next to me. Then again, maybe I was just easily flattered.

Ken reached over the dividing counsel and took my hand in his. "Karen, I haven't felt like this about another human being since

Melissa passed away." Melissa was Ken's wife, who'd died of breast cancer just over two years ago.

"No other human being, huh? But how about Baxter?" I knew I was using humor to deflect the intensity of his feelings. I just wasn't ready for that much openness. Ken gave me a wry smile acknowledging my need for space but making it clear he wasn't backing away.

It was probably just the trauma of the past few days making him talk that way, I told myself. Tragedy makes people reach out for the comfort of human connection. For some people, tragedy can pierce the hard shell they wear in daily life. That's some people. I just want to catch whoever's responsible and pin them to the wall!

"Now don't go all mushy on me," I said, kidding Ken. "Seriously, I think we should make the most of this event. Let's make a list of the people we should talk with," I said.

"O.K." Ken said, smoothly switching gears both figuratively and literally. "I'd say we should check out Carl Castoni. He'd benefit from Marvin's being gone. His vet practice will double."

"That's only true if they didn't have enough work for two vets. Since Marvin hired Carl, I'd think they had plenty of work, but we can check it out. And there's Norman Trout. Folks have said Norman had it in for Marvin because Marvin fired him," I said.

"I suppose Norman might have been angry but he did get a new job with Brie," Ken said.

"Yeah, and look what happened to her. Maybe Norman's some sort of psychopath," I said.

"Maybe, but it could be that Brie was the one who cut Marvin's parachute rip cord and then killed herself," Ken said. If that's the case, I don't know how we'll ever find out for sure."

"Well, I don't know what to believe—yet," I said.

"Well, then, here's another possibility. What about Clay Castoni? Starting up a vineyard's an expensive undertaking. No harvest for the first five years or so. And Carl is his brother's financial backer. Maybe Clay killed Marvin so his brother's veterinary practice would take off and Carl would have the money to back the vineyard," Ken postulated.

"O.K. that's possible, but we have the same caveat I brought up with Carl. Carl's only better off if the veterinary practice wasn't growing as they'd expected and Carl wanted it all for himself," I said. "So we have Clay, Carl, Brie and Norman as possible suspects. Any other folks we should check out?" I asked.

"Well, we should find out more about the trainers, Red Hamish and Harry Henry," Ken said.

"Yes, especially Red Hamish. You know, all this happened the weekend he arrived," I said.

"True," Ken said. "Very true. But did Marvin and Brie know Red Hamish before this weekend?" Ken asked.

"Well, as I understand it, this horse show is an annual event. So they could have met here last year or maybe at other shows around the country," I said.

"That's something we should ask about," Ken said.

"How about if we split up at the party? You check out Carl and Red, and I'll see what more I can learn about Clay, Norman and Harry," I suggested.

"Hmm... I'll check out Norman," Ken said. "I don't like the idea of you talking to Norman alone. You just said, to use your words, 'maybe he's a psychopath. And he might be a killer," Ken added.

"O.K. You talk to Norman and the Castoni brothers and I'll talk to the two trainers," I said. "Then we can compare notes on the way home."

"Sounds like a plan, Tuppence," Ken said.

"Indeed it does, Tommy," I replied. I smiled at Ken's allusion to Agatha Christie's little known, husband and wife detective duo.

Before his time with the Coast Guard, Ken had been a professor of English Literature at Clarke College. We'd spent several gorgeous June afternoons on his boat, floating on the backwaters of the Mississippi River and reading mysteries together.

Ken pulled into the winery lot and my thoughts snapped back from boating expeditions to the case at hand. The winery was situated in an old farmhouse. It had been expertly converted to its new purpose. A large wrap-around veranda provided abundant outdoor seating. The aroma of grilling barbecue wafted through the air.

Ken held the front door open for me and we walked into the tasting room. This room had once been the dining room. Now, three tables were arranged with bottles of Galena Grapes wine and dozens of clear long stemmed wine glasses. It was an inviting sight.

A young winery employee in a black vest, black slacks and sky-blue shirt stood behind each table pouring samples. We joined the central table. So much for splitting up, I thought. Oh well, we could do that in a minute.

The young woman serving wine greeted us and asked, "Would you prefer a red or a white wine?"

"What would you recommend?" I asked.

"If you want to try both, which is what I'd recommend, start with the lightest wine and move on to the heartiest," she replied.

"All right," I said, placing my fingertips on the stem of the wine glass in front of me.

"I'm Mary," the young woman said as she poured a half inch of Galena Grapes Chardonnay into each of our glasses. Feel free to ask me any questions you have about our wines," she offered.

"This is very buttery," I said, tossing out one of the wine terms I'd picked up at a wine tasting event at the new Goldmoor Inn restaurant just off Blackjack Road.

"We age our Chardonnay in oak barrels," Mary said. "That's what gives the wine that smooth buttery taste. Have a cracker to clear your palette and I'll pour you the Burgundy," Mary said, nodding to the large bowl of unsalted crackers on the table.

"I'll join you in one of those glasses," a man standing behind us said with a pronounced southern drawl.

We both turned to see Red Hamish sans his entourage.

"Please do," Ken said. "Where are your riders this afternoon?"

"The girls are a bit too young for the wine tasting. They'll be here for the dinner and the music afterwards though," Red said.

"Well, here's to Marvin and Brie," Ken said. Red's eyebrows shot up. He raised his glass.

"Indeed. To two people lost in the prime of youth," Red said.

"Not lost. Taken," Ken said.

Red nodded. "By the devil on horseback," Red said.

I looked at him questioningly, wondering if this was some old southern saying.

"Someone in our horse world is responsible for this," Red said. "Mark my words."

And I did. "Do you have any idea who?" I asked.

"I do. But it's just a feeling, you know. No proof at all. So my mouth is closed but my eyes are open. And that's my advice to you both, as well," Red Hamish said.

"Sound advice," Ken said. "But if you'll excuse me, Red, would you be so kind as to keep Karen company? I need to speak with someone for a moment."

"Of course, I'd be delighted," Red said.

"I'll catch up with you before dinner is served," Ken said as he gave me a kiss on the cheek.

I nodded my acknowledgement and then turned my attention to Red. "So, tell me. Did you know Marvin and Brie well?" I asked him.

"Knew them both, but just from last year's show here. Marvin was the veterinary for the show," Red said. "Now, Brie, everyone on this circuit knew Brie," Red snorted. "She let you know she was there."

"Was anyone angry with her or Marvin?" I asked.

"Oh, if you're asking who would have done this, well, the riders' money is on her groom right now. Anger you know—Marvin firing him and all. Maybe Brie figured that out and the fellow killed her too," Red said.

"I heard that it looked like she had taken an overdose of drugs," I said.

"That's what they were saying around the stables. Adam was there when Detective Cavanaugh and the coroner arrived. So he got to hear what they said. They think it could have been accidental, or a suicide, or even another murder. She had a bruise on her head that could have happened when she collapsed. Or, someone could have hit her on the head, knocked her out and then injected the drugs into her arm," Red said.

"Wow. And you think Norman could have done that?" I asked.

"Could have," Red replied.

"Do you know if he's here? Norman I mean. I'd like to talk to him," I said.

"I saw him with Very Harry when I came in," Red said.

"Very Harry?" I asked.

"Harry Henry. That's what I call him," Red said.

I gave a half smile but wondered about the animosity between those two men. "Thanks," I said, excusing myself. I put a tip in the jar on Mary's table and thanked her as well.

Out on the veranda, the late afternoon sun made me squint. As my eyes adjusted, I saw Harry talking to Roger Lesser just ten feet away. Roger had his back to the wall and Harry was pointing his finger right in Roger's face. They seemed quite engrossed in their conversation. Harry turned when he heard my steps coming toward him and Roger took the opportunity to slip away.

"Harry," I said, extending my hand. "Karen Prince."

"Oh, yes. I remember. Excuse me," he said dismissively and turned to follow Roger.

"Tragic about Brie. She was a client of yours, wasn't she?" I called after him. Harry stopped and turned back to look at me.

"Yes. But she obviously had a drug problem. She wasn't the easiest person to work with because of that," Harry said. "Still, as you said, it is tragic."

"Do you think it was an accidental overdose?" I asked.

"What else would it be?"

"Well, I heard it could have been intentional, either by her or someone." Harry's eyes narrowed and he ran his hand over his scraggly long hair. "No, she did this herself. I'm quite sure," he said.

"Were you with Brie this morning?" I asked.

"Of course. I'm her trainer. We met every morning when there was a show. We were getting ready for the first class of the day," Harry said.

"So you were with her Saturday morning too?" I asked.

"Yes, I just said. I was with her every morning of the show," Harry said.

"Did you by any chance see Marvin on Saturday morning?" I asked.

"No. Not at all," Harry said.

My forehead tingled again. There was something about that quick denial that troubled me. Something I'd heard that didn't fit. I just couldn't put my finger on what it was. It would come to me though. I was sure.

"Karen." I heard my name and turned to see Ken tapping me on the shoulder.

"Ken. Let me introduce you to Harry," I said. I turned but Harry was gone.

"What was that about?" Ken asked.

"I don't know," I said.

"Anyway, I came to get you for the winery tour. Clay's giving the tour now, before dinner." Ken took my hand and led us toward the side door of the winery. When we were well away from the other guests, Ken leaned in and whispered: "Can't be too careful. I have something I want to tell you. I heard Carl tell Clay he'd gotten an e-mail from a woman in Asheville looking for her horse," Ken said.

"Someone stole her horse?" I asked, matching Ken's whispering tone and wondering what he was talking about

"No. Apparently she'd sold the horse through an agent and doesn't know who the buyer was. But she thought the buyer was from Galena. So she sent an e-mail to both Carl and Marvin because they were the only two veterinarians who treated horses in the area. She figured one of them would know who'd bought her horse."

"And did Carl know?" I asked.

"No. He said he hadn't treated any new horses recently."

"So, was this an auction sale?" I asked.

"Carl didn't say. It could have been, I suppose," Ken said.

We were at the winery door now and joined the crowd in the tasting room. Clay spoke to the assembled group of about thirty people.

"Welcome," Clay said. "I'm glad you were all able to join me at the Galena Grapes Winery today. My brother, Carl, and I started this venture five years ago. We bought one hundred acres of land and planted two-year-old vines. We've tended them for the past five years and last fall we harvested our first grapes. We made five hundred bottles of wine last year and we intend to make eight hundred bottles this fall. We hand pick the grapes in late September. Follow me and we'll go into the wine making room."

Clay led the now quiet group from the tasting room into a large open room with a newly poured concrete floor. The room was lined with large oak barrels standing upright.

"We start the actual wine-making process by putting the grapes through a crusher. The crusher just breaks the skins on the grapes and drops the grapes and juice into these open barrels," Clay said. "The grapes sit in the barrels for about six days. The natural yeast on the outside of the grape skins comes into contact with the sugar in the grape juice. That starts the fermentation process.

"After six days, the juice has picked up a beautiful red color from the grape skins. Then we tap off the juice by opening the spigot at the base of each barrel. We put that juice into the fermenting barrels you see lying on their sides against the far wall. We strain the juice to catch any seeds as we pour the juice into the fermenting barrels.

"Then we go back to those original barrels that still have the stems and skins left in the bottom. We transfer that mixture to the press. That's the gadget over there that looks like a barrel with open slats," Clay said. We all followed Clay to the press. There was a sort of gutter around the bottom of the barrel with a funnel like opening. The press had a large metal wheel at the top and a crank handle at the side.

"We put the grape skins in here and turn this handle. That brings down the press which squeezes the remaining juice out of the skins. The juice runs out between the open slats and flows down into the gutter and is funneled into a transfer vessel.

"We add the juice from this pressing to the fermenting barrels and let that sit for several months. Now, notice the open hole on the top of the fermenting barrels? We fill the barrels to the top to minimize the surface area of the wine that comes in contact with the air. But we don't close up that hole. Can anyone tell me why?" Clay asked.

One of the women riders spoke up. "Because the wine is still fermenting," she said.

"Exactly right," Clay responded. "The wine continues to bubble away. In fact, we build a cement dam around the hole so that, as the wine bubbles during the fermentation process, the dam walls will keep the wine from running down the sides of the barrel."

"How long does the fermentation process go on?" one of the gentlemen in the group asked Clay.

"Usually about six or eight weeks. Once the alcohol level in the wine reaches fourteen percent it will kill the yeast and the fermentation stops naturally," Clay said.

"Do you add anything to the wine?" another person in the group asked.

"We make a completely natural wine here," Clay said. We don't add any preservatives and we never add sugar. We just continue to top off the barrel with the grape juice as the barrel soaks up some of the wine over those six weeks.

"When the fermentation process stops, we cork up the barrel, remove the cement dam and let the wine age for three more months. Then it's on to the bottling room. Follow me," Clay said.

We walked out of the pressing and fermenting room and followed Clay into another cement floored room. "This is our bottling area. The bottling is all done by machine. We place the bottles in here and they go through this sterilization chamber. Then the bottles are cooled, filled with wine and capped," Clay said.

"Did you say capped?" a gentleman asked.

"Yes. The latest trend among vintners is to use metal caps on wine bottles instead of corks. Did you know that seven percent of all wine is spoiled by the interaction of the wine with the cork? Natural cork can impart an off flavor to the wine and we say it's been 'corked'. That's why the sommelier at a fine restaurant will allow you to taste the wine and inspect the cork before he pours wine for the table," Clay said.

"So, by switching to metal caps you avoid that problem," the gentleman said.

"Precisely," Clay responded. "Once the wine has been bottled, we let it rest on its side in the storage racks in the wine cellar. I'll show you that next."

The group followed Clay down a stairway into a limestone walled cellar. Floor to ceiling wine racks stood in rows along the perimeter of the room.

"This is the original basement. Being underground the temperature stays close to fifty-five degrees year round. That's the perfect temperature for storing wine. That's how we make wine here at Galena Grapes Winery," Clay said.

There was a round of applause which resounded against the limestone walls. "Let's all go up and have some dinner," Clay said.

We all followed Clay back up the wooden stairs, through the tasting room and out onto the broad veranda. Six tables for six were set on the veranda with long white table cloths and floral centerpieces. It was an elegant sight, all the more dramatic against the backdrop of the rolling farmland and vineyard plantings surrounding the winery. I saw Dara Brown already seated at one of the tables and she waved me over saying, "Karen, come join us."

Dara and her husband, Raymond Brown, were seated with Harry Henry and Roger Lesser. As we took our seats, Dara acted as hostess and introduced us to everyone around the table. I'd met Henry at the stables and Roger at the Antique Art Show, but Ken had not. Following the introductions, conversation quickly turned to Brie.

"What an awful shock you had this morning, Harry," Raymond Brown said. My ears perked up.

"Yes, I was supposed to meet Brie at the stables to get ready for the show. I got there early to saddle Elvis and there she was lying on the floor in the stable. I thought she was sleeping or something, but when I called to wake her up she didn't move. I bent over and shook her shoulder and she was stone cold," Harry said.

"How awful!" I said. Ken put his hand on my knee under the table in a comforting gesture. "Was anyone else around that might have seen what happened?" I asked.

"There were a few other people in the stables. Roger, you were there, weren't you?" Harry asked.

Roger glared at Harry. "Yes, I was getting my own horse ready for the day's ride," Roger said.

"Did you see anyone with Brie?" Ken asked Roger.

"I didn't see Brie at all. My stall is just a few stalls away from hers but I didn't hear a thing."

"Would you have heard her if she'd been talking to someone?" I asked. I didn't know how far sound traveled there, but it was probably not too hard to overhear what was going on a few stalls away. I thought of how Carl had overheard my conversation with Polly in her stall on Saturday.

"Yes. It was pretty quiet at that time of the morning and if she'd had someone else in her stall I would have heard them," Roger said.

"What will happen to Elvis?" Dara asked.

"Elvis is a gorgeous horse. I suppose I'll have to sell him for the estate. Are you interested in another horse?" Harry asked Dara.

"I don't know. Maybe. I'll think about that. And what about Brie's new horse, Goldie? How is she doing? I heard she was pretty ill," Dara said.

"She is. I don't know. I suppose Brie's mother will have to decide how much she's willing to do for that horse. Care is very expensive," Harry said.

"So Brie's mother is her executrix?" I asked.

"I'm guessing she is," Harry said. "Even though she's in New York, she is the only family that Brie has."

"I suppose she'll be flying out here," Dara said. "I'll have to give her a call."

"Do you know Brie's mother?" I asked Dara.

"It's a small town. We met when she was living here years ago and raising Brie. She could stay with us but I'm leaving for the Biltmore in a few days."

"You too! I'll be there as well. And I heard Sassy Ballantine is going. Harry and Roger, are you both going to the Biltmore show?" I asked.

Harry answered first. "Yes, I have some clients there that are looking for a new horse. We're talking about taking a trip to Austria and looking at some horses there. We're meeting at the Grand Prix dinner to make the final arrangements."

"Austria, how exciting! And Roger, are you going?"

"I think I will," he said. "Sounds like the place to be."

"Not to change the subject, but how did the Art Museum and the Historical Society do at the Antique Art Show yesterday?" I asked.

"The turn-out was better than we expected and everyone was very happy about having their paintings displayed and learning more about them," Dara said. "Especially Liz!"

"That was incredible! She really had no idea what a treasure she had there," I said.

"Yes, imagine having an original Heade hanging in your home all those years and not knowing it! It's lucky nothing ever happened to it!" Roger said.

"I saw another incredible painting yesterday," I added before I'd really thought about what I was saying. "Lynne has an original George Catlin Indian painting in her home." As the words left my lips it occurred to me that Lynne might not want people to know she had such a valuable painting hanging in her home. Oops!

Roger looked at me. "Really, I'll have to talk to her about that. What sort of painting is it?" Roger asked.

"It's an oil portrait of a tribal chief," I replied.

"You never know what you're going to find hidden away here in Galena do you?" Dara said. "I think we'll have to repeat this Antique Art Show idea next year. After Liz's find, more people will want to bring in their old paintings to see what they have. Don't you think so?" Dara asked me.

"Yes, I think it's a great idea," I said.

Clay's staff served a wonderful barbecue dinner. The event wrapped up about 9:00 p.m. just as the summer sun was setting. The drive home was all the more gorgeous in the warm twilight. Ken had dropped me off and headed home by 9:30 p.m.

Chapter Ten

Talking Points

Truffles licked my hand and nestled into the crook of my arm. I looked at my watch—7:00 a.m. Ughh! I hadn't had much sleep. The events of the past few days had me shaken. I'd woken myself with nightmares three times last night. In the last one I was at Galena Stables running from ring to ring. Brie was riding Elvis jumping through blazing hoops. A hot air balloon exploded overhead in an echoing "ka-boom" and fell in flames to the ground. Every time I'd startled myself awake I'd tossed and turned trying to think of who had killed Marvin and Brie. Could Brie really have killed Marvin and then taken her own life? I suppose it was possible. What were the chances of there being two unrelated deaths at the same place in the same week? It seemed more likely the same person was responsible for killing them both.

So, what tied the two of them together? They'd dated, but that was almost two years ago. They both rode horses but so did a lot of other people. These thoughts were still whirling through my mind as I slipped out of bed, leaving Truffs snuggled on the bed covers.

That didn't last long. Before I'd gotten ten steps from the bed Truffles had awoken from her own kitty dreams. She meowed, bounded from the bed and pranced around my ankles as if to say, "Good morning! How about breakfast?"

"Well, all right. Let's go downstairs!" I said as I petted her. Truffs padded along after me as I made my way down the stairs to the kitchen. I gave Truffs her breakfast and poured myself a cup of strong black brew. I sipped this wondrous elixir as I walked into the living room. The red light on my answering machine caught my eye. I hadn't noticed it blinking last night when I came home but it must have been. I pressed the play button and listened. "Karen, this is Lynne Shaw. I was hiking yesterday and found some gorgeous Indian points by that old brewery we were looking at yesterday. I was wondering if you'd like to go for a hike tomorrow and I'll show you where I found them and what to look for on your own hikes. Give me a call if this sounds good."

It did sound good! Lynne must have called when I was at the winery yesterday, so she was talking about hiking today. Excellent. I wanted to spend a little time in the studio with "Pansy Orchid" but that would only take a few hours. Even when I think I've finished a painting I look at it over the next few days to see what more I can do to refine it. Tiny adjustments: a fine line to emphasize a petal's edge, the shadow under a tiny dew drop, these little details make a huge difference in the overall effect of a painting. Duly fortified with coffee and my feline friend fed and watered, I returned upstairs and did my twenty minutes of floor exercises and twenty minutes on the hamster wheel (a/k/a the Stairmaster). I listened to my computer read the New York Times front page as I huffed and puffed. Country life certainly was more interesting with a satellite internet connection.

It was 8 a.m. by the time I was showered and dressed. That seemed a reasonable time to call Lynne. She answered on the first ring and we made plans to meet at her place at noon. That gave me a good three hours of studio time. Perfect!

Just one more call to make. 8:00 a.m. here was 9:00 a.m. in New York. That's way too early for the average New Yorker to be at the office and Marshall was no exception. But I figured I could catch him on his cell. He'd probably be having coffee somewhere. As it turned out, I caught him walking through Central Park on his way to a coffee shop. "Marshall! It's Karen. I got your message the other day and I have good news! "Pansy Orchid is just about done!"

"Karen! That is great news! I can't wait to see it. Send me an e-mail with the image as soon as you can," Marshall said.

"I will. It should be ready to ship in a few weeks. I'll let it dry for a week, and then put a final glaze finish on it. It'll be ready to frame in another week after that."

"So, it sounds like I'll have it in about three weeks. That'll give me time to get some good photographs and get it into our brochure for the show. Perfect!"

"How's the show coming along?" I asked.

"Looks like we'll have a wonderful kickoff for the holiday season. I'll have twenty-five new works by our gallery artists," Marshall said. "I'm doing a four-color glossy book featuring all the paintings in the show and details from some of the more complex works. It should be about thirty pages and it'll be gorgeous! Even better than last year, judging by the digital images I've been getting," Marshall said.

"What day will the opening be?"

"November 30th. Will you be able to come?"

"Wouldn't miss your biggest show of the year! Of course, I'll be there. The Rembrandt show will be on at the Met then. I'll enjoy seeing that, as well. And the stores will all be decorated for the holidays; it'll be a great weekend!" I said.

"Why don't you spend the week? Take your time. Do the galleries. I'll show you some great little restaurants!"

"That's tempting. Let me think about that and I'll get back to you. All right?"

"Of course, my dear. Of course! Just know I'd be happy to be your tour guide."

"You'll have a million things to do with the show going on!" I said.

"That's true. But, one has to eat, right? We can always have dinners."

"Well, that's a few months off. We don't have to make plans quite yet. First thing is to finish the painting for you!"

"I thought it was done!"

"Nearly, Marshall. Very nearly. Just a few finishing touches! You'll see. I'll send you a photo today, I promise."

"All right! I'll look for it! Well, I'm at the coffee shop by the gallery now. Nice walking and talking with you!"

"Good to talk to you too, Marshall. I'll e-mail you with the delivery info when I ship the painting. You'll let me know when it arrives safe and sound, won't you?"

"Of course I will. I always do, don't I?" Marshall said.

"Yes, you do. And I appreciate knowing my paintings are in such good hands with you!"

"You know I'll take very good care of them," Marshall said.

"O.K. Well, I'd best go. Talk to you soon," I said.

"Bye for now," Marshall said and rang off.

The hours flew by in my studio, per usual. At 11:00 a.m. I washed my brushes and arranged them on their drying towel, then covered them with a clean lint free cloth so they'd be ready for my next painting session. I was already in jeans and jogging shoes, which I figured would do fairly well as hiking clothes. So, I checked on Truffs, grabbed two bottles of water and headed out to Lynne's in the Boxster.

It was just before noon when I pulled up in front of Lynne's house. She was crouched in front of the bridal bushes in her front yard, spreading mulch.

"Hi! I see you're a gardener too!" I said.

"I love spending an hour out here when I can. The gardens are really pretty well established. So it's mostly a matter of keeping the weeds at bay. And that seems to be a never ending job!" Lynne said.

"Well, your gardens look great! Are you still up for a hike?" I asked.

"You bet! Let me just toss this stuff in the garage and I'll be ready," Lynne said, scooping up the half bag of mulch and the rake lying next to it.

I toured Lynne's front garden for a few minutes while I waited for her. Two island flower beds flanked the sides of Lynne's lot. Red daylilies with deep yellow throats filled the beds with strong color. Tall double yellow hollyhocks stood behind the daylilies echoing the colors in the daylilies.

Lynne returned with keys in her hands. "Why don't we take my jeep and we can drive over to the brewery and start our hike from there," Lynne suggested.

"Sounds good to me. Lead on," I said.

We headed north on Highway 20 over the Galena River Bridge. Lynne jogged left on Main, right on Gear Street and in a few blocks took a left on Ferry Landing Road.

In a few minutes we were out of the city. Lynne turned left on Old Brewer's Lane, a dirt road running along the Galena River across from the trail we'd jogged on Sunday.

"You know, I don't think I've ever been back here," I said.

"Oh, you'll love hiking back here. It's all State Preserve Land. A lot of it was owned by the Jensen's. When they passed away, about twenty years ago, they left it to the State with the provision that it be kept as a preserve. Our local Natural Area Guardians put in the parking area. You'll see it in a minute. The trail follows the river through some gorgeous areas then comes out at the Mississippi. There are a couple of old buildings back here that have been abandoned," Lynne said. There hasn't been too much building out here because the Galena River floods the lower lying land in the spring. When the ice melt raises the Mississippi it raises the level of the Galena River as well.

We bounced along on the rutted dirt road. After about a mile, Lynne pulled the jeep into a small gravel parking area lined with large limestone boulders. "This is it," Lynne said. "I can't believe you've never been out here!"

Tall oak, hickory and black walnut trees lined the parking lot. As soon as we got out of the car, Lynne sprayed herself with two layers of bug repellent and offered them to me.

"This one's Avon Skin-so-Soft, for the gnats. And this one's Deet, for the ticks and mosquitoes," she said.

After we were double sprayed, we headed out into the woods along the north side of the Galena River. Despite the parking area, this was clearly an unofficial trail. The path was only a foot wide and appeared to be used more by deer and turkey than by people. But it was gorgeous. We walked west for a about a mile in silence, enjoying the sights and sounds of the woods. Birds chirped, butterflies flew by and leaves rustled as squirrels scampered along the tree branches. Lynne stopped and pointed to a huge limestone outcropping on our right, about fifty feet off the trail. "Come on this way," she said and headed off the trail toward the rocks.

A wall of gray limestone rocks rose thirty feet above us. Moss grew on the sides of the rock and I noticed a small cavern at the base of the rocks. Lynne walked to the edge of the rock and crouched down. "Here, look at this," she said. Lynne picked up what looked like a triangular rock and held it out to me.

"What's this?" I asked, holding a roughly two inch wide by two inch long, cream colored rock in my hand. One edge of the rock came to a point and it seemed natural to orient the point upward. The side opposite of the point, the bottom, narrowed to form an inch wide base. I turned the rock sideways and noticed that the width of the rock tapered from a very narrow on the point to about three-quarters inch wide at the base. The two sides of the rock were quite different from one another. One was smooth and convex. The other side was rough, with a pointed ridge down the center.

I was wondering if this could have naturally chipped off a larger rock in this form when Lynne said, "Take a really close look at the pointed edge of that rock. What do you see?"

I stepped into a shaft of light that pierced the tree canopy. Holding the rock up close to my eyes I noticed that the leading edge of the rock was formed by eighth of an inch long chips which made a sort of fluted edge. The edge came to a point and the ridge that ran vertically down the center of the rough side of the rock ran exactly to the center of the pointed edge. I didn't think that could be a coincidence.

Is this some sort of arrow head?" I asked. "It's a lot wider and thicker than any arrowhead I've ever seen."

"I'd say that's a large hunting point. It would have been attached to a spear and thrown or jabbed into the prey animal. And look here," she said, crouching again. In the soil was another smaller but similarly shaped rock. "These points are made from chert, a sort or strong whitish rock that formed in the cavities of the limestone rock. I'll bet the Indians came here to find chert and made their points right here," Lynne said.

"Wow! How long ago do you think that would have been?" I asked.

"Oh, I'd say these are late Woodland or early Mississippian period, roughly 1,000 years ago."

"That's amazing!" I said.

"Have you been to the Chapman Site by Hanover?" Lynne asked.

"No, but I did hear they'd excavated an Indian village there."

"Yes. They found artifacts from the Woodland and Mississippian periods there too. They think the Indians did some trading with the Cahokians."

"Who were the Cahokians?" I asked.

"Cahokia was an Indian Village just east of East St. Louis, Illinois. Nine hundred years ago, about 1100 A.D., Cahokia was a city of about five thousand people. It was the center of a political and trade network of communities up and down the Mississippi River. The city itself was a series of neighborhoods, each with a prominent flat-topped mound. The most prominent citizen of each neighborhood had their house on the top of the mound. The center of the city was enclosed by a log stockade. There were twenty-foot tall logs, lined-up side by side, to make an impenetrable wall. Inside the wall there was a large open plaza and a few neighborhoods. The largest mound is called Monks Mound, at the north end of the plaza. It's over one hundred feet tall, eight hundred feet wide, and one thousand feet long at its base. There was a huge building at the top of that mound and archeologists think that was the home of the Cahokians' leader," Lynne said.

"That's a huge city. I had no idea we had such complex Indian cities here in the Midwest. Whatever happened to them?" I asked.

"Well, we don't know why, but the Cahokians abandoned the city about seven hundred years ago. Archaeologists think they may just have depleted the resources of the area."

"And the people living in this area may have traded with them? That's fascinating. I wonder why we don't hear more about Midwestern Indians. Sounds like they had quite a complex civilization. But you only hear about the Native American Indians living out West."

"I don't know. But I find it fascinating!" Lynne said. "Come on. Let's hike a little ways more. You remember that old brewery building we saw on our jog on Sunday?"

"Sure," I said.

"Well, there's a great spring that comes out of the hillside right next to it that I'd like to show you. I've found some incredible scrapers in the stream that flows down to the river from that spring," Lynne said.

We made our way back through the knee high undergrowth to the foot trail. In another quarter mile a dirt road crossed the trail.

"This is the road that leads from the brewery building to the Galena River. It connects back to Ferry Road a ways past the brewery," Lynne said. "Want to go check it out?"

"I would, actually. And I'd like to see if the boxes those kayakers were carrying are still there!" I said. "I thought that was weird, didn't you?"

"Yea, sort of. I thought maybe they were setting up for a camp-out or something," Lynne said.

"By kayak?" I asked.

"Who knows? Maybe they just live on the river and like kayaking."

"I suppose," I said but I wasn't really convinced.

The road looked like it might once have been gravel, but it was pretty much hard packed, rutted dirt now. Branches hung over the sides and weeds grew up here and there. But it wasn't entirely overgrown, so it must still have gotten some use. The road rose at a steady incline. When we got to the top the land leveled out for a bit and the old orange brick brewery building came into sight about a quarter mile ahead.

When we got within a hundred yards I thought I heard voices coming from the direction of the brewery. I put my hand on Lynne's arm, stopped and put my index finger to my lips in the age old sign for silence. She looked at me questioningly and I pointed to the brewery and cupped my ear with my right hand. She got the idea and we both strained to listen for a minute. There it was again. Louder this time.

Two male voices were clearly discernable now. "I told you I left it right here!"

"Yeah, sure. So where is it?"

"I don't know. It was here Sunday night."

"I'm not paying you and you'd better come up with the stuff this week. Got it?" one of the voices said. He sounded angry.

Lynne motioned me to the side of the road. Staying close to the trees we crept toward the brewery to get a better look. Two men in jeans and tee shirts stood face to face next to the door of the abandoned brewery. The first fellow was huge, probably two hundred and fifty pounds and a good six foot two. The second fellow was smaller, shorter and, hey, he looked a lot like Norman Trout! Could that be him, I wondered. What would he be doing out here?

I gave Lynne a quizzical look and whispered, "I think I recognize that shorter guy. Isn't that Norman Trout, Brie's stable hand?"

Lynne's eyebrows shot up and she nodded her head. I crooked my index finger in a "follow me" gesture, crouched down and crept up closer.

There was a clearing around the old building and we stopped just short of the edge of the woods. We were within thirty feet of the two men now. Lynne and I left the road and crept into the underbrush and peered at the men from our leafy hideout. We stood behind a thicket of raspberry bushes and mulberry trees. The larger guy had a beard, a shaved head and huge muscular arms poking out from his sleeveless tee-shirt. The muscular man shoved Norman and sent him sprawling to the ground. Norman lay there gasping and the other fellow put his foot on Norman's chest and said, "This happens again and next time you won't get up. You got that?"

Norman raised himself up on one elbow and nodded. "Meet me here Thursday and I'll have it all for you."

"You better not be wasting any more of my time. You're holding up the whole operation," he said and then spat on the ground, turned and walked away. Just then a deer leapt across the lane and jumped into the woods within five feet of us! Both men turned towards us.

"What was that?" the tee-shirt guy asked. Norman was up now and they both stood looking in our direction.

"Probably a deer," Norman said.

The larger guy didn't seem so convinced. He stood staring for another minute. My heart pounded and adrenaline coursed through my veins. One thought ran through my head: Do not come over here. Do not come over here. We stood stock-still.

"Thursday," the big guy said to Norman and then turned and walked away. He must have been parked behind the building because a minute later he was driving off in a red pick-up truck. Norman waited for the fellow to leave and then pulled a cell phone out of his pocket.

"Yeah, it's me. We have a problem. The stuff wasn't here! He just left but I set it up again for Thursday. Same time, same place."

"I have no idea. I left it here Sunday and it's not here now. That's all I know. Someone else must have known about this."

"No, no. It couldn't have been kids. No one comes out here. And even if they did, I didn't just leave it out in the open. It was in an old cabinet in the ice cellar. We better put some eyes on this place from now until Thursday. Yeah, see you."

Norman clicked his phone shut and headed to the back of the building. A minute later he drove away in a black pickup.

"What do you think that was about?" I asked Lynne.

"I don't know. Sounded like a drug deal or something," she said.

"Yeah, I thought so too. Come on, let's go take a peek inside," I whispered.

"Go in the brewery? Are you crazy? What if they come back?" Lynne said in a high pitched whisper.

"Why would they? They said they'd be back on Thursday. Come on," I said and then crept out of the woods toward the old brick building. Lynne hesitated and then I heard her footsteps behind me.

We stopped at the doorway, looked around and listened. I didn't hear anything except my heart pounding in my chest. I guess I was a little bit worried about those guys coming back too. I pulled up the bottom of my running shirt and used it to turn the knob on the old door. "Fingerprints," I whispered to Lynne in response to her quizzical look. I gave the door a push and stepped inside.

Light filtered in through the openings where windows once had been. Broken glass and empty beer cans were scattered around the filthy floor. I scanned the room and saw a stairway at the far side. "The ice cellar Norman talked about must be down there," I whispered to Lynne. "Come on. Or you could wait here and be the look-out," I said.

"The look-out! I thought you just told me they wouldn't be back until Thursday," Lynne said with something near hysteria in her voice.

"Oh, come on," I said, motioning Lynne to follow me as I stepped around scattered debris on my way to the stairs.

The basement looked dark. A dank odor wafted up the stairs. Maybe this wasn't such a good idea after all, I thought. Then I remembered the penlight my friend Wanda had given me. I reached into my pocket, pulled out my keys and clicked on the little light attached to them. That was enough to steel my resolve. The first stair creaked under my weight. Lynne followed closely in the little beam of my light. Amazing how often that little gadget came in handy! I mentally sent Wanda a "thank-you."

I was beginning to wonder how we'd see anything in this basement. Then, at the base of the stairs, my penlight flashed on something tall and metallic. A floodlight! I flicked on the switch and the battery powered light lit up an area about thirty feet ahead of us. A wooden cabinet stood against the near wall. Cobwebs ran from the wall to the cabinet top. I made my way to the old cabinet while Lynne waited on the bottom stair. The cabinet was about five feet high, about two feet deep, and had its doors slightly ajar.

"This must be where Norman had the stuff stashed," I said in a stage whisper. I used the edge of my keys to swing open one of the cabinet doors. Empty! The thick layer of dust on the middle shelf had been disturbed.

"Nothing in here," I said to Lynne in a low voice.

"Fine! Let's get out of here!" Lynne said, then turned and started up the stairs. Suddenly there was loud crash. Lynne's scream echoed through the stone basement. The middle stair had given way! Lynne's left foot and ankle had gone right through the old rotten wood. She'd caught herself on the railing which was now taking the brunt of her weight.

"Oh, Lynne! Are you all right?" I made my way gingerly up the stairs to her. My penlight showed jagged wooden splinters around her calf. "Can you move your foot?" I asked.

"I don't know. I'll try," Lynne said. I stood on the stair below her and slipped my arm under her right shoulder to help support her weight.

"I can wiggle my toes," Lynne said tentatively. "And I can move my ankle."

"That's good! O.K. Now, brace your weight on the stair above you. I want to get more light on you," I said. Once Lynne had her right foot on the next stair, I ran back down and directed the floodlight at her. I worked to remove the splintered wood around Lynne's calf so she could extricate her foot without being impaled on the jagged edges. I didn't want to think about Norman or "the bruiser" coming back while we were trapped like this, but I couldn't think of anything else. Finally, Lynne's leg was free and we got the heck out of there!

We made it back to the woods and took a look at Lynne's leg. It was bruised and scratched, but the cuts weren't deep. Good thing she'd been wearing jeans. And even a better thing that no bones were broken!

"Are you sure you can walk all right?" I asked.

"I'm sure," Lynne said. "I'm just bruised."

"O.K." I said. "If you're sure."

"Come on. We can take the road back to my car. It makes a loop back to Ferry Road, and then to Highway 20," Lynne said.

Another twenty minute hike and we were back at the parking lot where we'd left Lynne's car. "Hey, do you think they noticed our car?" I asked. "If they think someone was out here stealing their stuff, they might have gotten your license plate!" I said.

Lynne looked at me and wrinkled up her nose. "I sure hope not!" she said.

"Me too! That fellow didn't look like he was kidding around," I said. "In fact, I think I'll call Detective Cavanaugh right now."

"That sounds like a really good idea!" Lynne said.

As Lynne drove us back to her place, I called Detective Cavanaugh and got his answering machine. Darn! I didn't know what to say, exactly, so I just left a message asking him to call me as soon as he could.

"I think he'll call back when he gets that. But, I suppose I'll see him tomorrow at Marvin's funeral service. I hate to go to those things, but I will. Are you going?" I asked Lynne.

"Can't. I have to be in Rockford," Lynne said.

"I just thought of something," I said. "We left that floodlight on!"

"Are you saying you want to go back?" Lynne exclaimed nearly driving off the road when she turned to look at me.

"No! I'm just saying, we left the light on!"

"Well, tell Detective Cavanaugh about that too!" Lynne said. She was rapidly losing her sense of humor.

In a few minutes we were back at Lynne's place and the Boxster was there waiting for me. As Lynne pulled up to the curb to let me out I noticed something odd.

"Hey Lynne, did you leave your front door open?"

"No, why?" she asked, bending down and looking at me through the opened passenger side door. That was when she saw the broken glass. The glass panel that flanked Lynne's front door was smashed.

I looked from the open front door back to Lynne and said, "You'd better park out here. I'm calling Detective Cavanaugh again! Someone broke in your house while we were gone!"

Chapter Eleven

Missing Masterpiece

This time I got through to Detective Cavanaugh on the first ring. "Cavanaugh," his voice boomed through my tiny phone.

"This is Karen Prince, Detective,"

He cut me off. "Karen, I just got your message. What's all this about?"

My mind whirled. My message? Oh, right. "My message was about something else. I mean, I saw something I have to tell you about, but I'm calling about something else," I babbled. "Wait, let me start again." I was flustered and I hated that. I knew I wasn't making any points. I took a deep, calming breath and continued, "I'm standing in front of Lynne Shaw's place and someone just broke in," I said relatively calmly.

"Just broke in! Did you see them? Are they still there?" he asked in rapid fire succession.

"We didn't see them, but the door's open, and a window's broken. We were only gone about an hour, so it had to have just happened. I don't know if they're still inside or not," I said.

"What's the address? I'll be right there. Do not, I repeat, do not attempt to apprehend this person. Do not go into the house. Stay right there. Got that?"

"Got it!" I gave Detective Cavanaugh the Park Avenue address and clicked my phone shut.

Lynne was out of her jeep and standing next to me now. "Cavanaugh will be here in a minute. He wants us to wait for him right here, just in case someone's still inside," I said. Lynne nodded.

The Sheriff's Department is just across the Galena River, on the north side of Bench Street. I'd been to the jail a few years ago when my friend, Alice, had been wrongly detained. That was the first time I'd met Detective Cavanaugh. I'd helped find the people who'd been responsible for Alice's ex's murder. And, although I am sure Detective Cavanaugh was glad to have apprehended the criminals in that case, I don't think he'd been too happy with my involvement. Which, come to think of it, was probably why he'd been so insistent on my waiting for him outside. But honestly, I had no intention of going into a house that might have a burglar inside!

Lynne and I leaned on her jeep staring at her open front door for the three minutes it took Detective Cavanaugh to arrive. Neither of us saw any signs of movement in the house, as we told Detective Cavanaugh. He got a quick description of the house's lay-out from Lynne and then told us to wait where we were. Cavanaugh drew his gun from his hip holster, grasped the gun with both hands and walked up the front walkway.

At the front door, Cavanaugh pressed his back against the door jam, peered into the living room and disappeared inside. Lynne and I looked at each other and waited in tense silence for some sign from Cavanaugh. A few minutes later and Cavanaugh came around from the back of the house. "Nothing seems disturbed except the front door. Back door was still locked," he said. "I'd like you to come in and take a look around. Tell me if you see anything out of place that I might have missed."

"Don't touch anything. I want to get some finger prints around this door," Cavanaugh said as he led the way into the house.

We went inside with Detective Cavanaugh leading the way. Even though he'd gone through the house before we went in, it was still creepy knowing someone had broken in. Could they still be hiding in there somewhere? Lynne must have felt even more nervous. She walked gingerly around her small living room. Suddenly, she stopped and gasped. There was an empty space on the wall where the George Catlin Indian Chief portrait had hung.

I followed her gaze and gasped as well. "Someone knew what they were doing," I said. "This is no ordinary burglary."

"What? What do you mean?" Detective Cavanaugh asked looking from one of us to the other.

"I had a rather costly painting hanging there, Detective Cavanaugh. Not many people who saw it would have known what it was. I made a point not to mention it to anyone," Lynne said.

I flushed guiltily. Hadn't I mentioned it at dinner at the winery last night? But heavens, I hadn't thought it was a secret. And who'd I mentioned it to anyway? Just Dara and she certainly wasn't a thief. She could afford to buy her own Catlin if she wanted one anyway. Who'd been sitting around us that could have overheard our conversation, I wondered. But my thoughts were interrupted.

"Do you have a photo of the painting?" Detective Cavanaugh asked.

"Yes, I do. Let me get it for you," Lynne said. She went to her desk and pulled out a manila file. "These are photos of every room in the house. I took them last year for my insurance files."

"So this art work is insured?" Cavanaugh asked.

"Yes, of course," Lynne said. "I'll have to call them. Can you give me a copy of your report when you have it Detective?"

"Yes, but let's go through the rest of the house."

We went room by room but nothing else had been disturbed. This thief had a single purpose and that fits," Cavanaugh said.

"Fits with what?" Lynne asked.

"We had another art theft last night," Cavanaugh said.

"What! In Galena? What was stolen?" I asked and my mind immediately flashed to Sunday's Art Show. Lynne had I locked eyes. She'd obviously had the same thought.

"An old flower painting by an artist named Heade. It was stolen from Liz Seelig's home last night," Cavanaugh said. "She said you identified the painting for her at the Art Show on Sunday," Cavanaugh said, looking at me.

"Yes, I did. We had a fundraiser event at the Historical Society and I guess everyone there heard this was a valuable painting," I said.

"Everyone there and everyone they told! In this town, word travels fast," Detective Cavanaugh said. "Did you mention this Catlin painting at that event? Think carefully, it might have been natural to come up in conversation at a show like that," Detective Cavanaugh asked us.

"I didn't even know about Lynne's painting until after the Art Show," I said. "We came back here and that was the first time I saw it." Then I flushed and added, "But I think I might have mentioned it at the winery event last night," I confessed. Lynne looked at me. "Well, I was just talking to Dara," I said, defensively.

"I'll need a list of everyone at that event and everyone who might have overheard your conversation," Detective Cavanaugh said. "O.K. How about you, Lynne? Who comes in here and would have known about this painting?"

"Well, I have a cleaning lady of course. And a bug-spray guy. And the security alarm people. The lawn guy could have come in once or twice, I suppose. And I guess I did have book club here a month or so ago. And, I have an annual drop in holiday party," Lynne said.

"O.K. So, this painting wasn't really a secret, I guess," Detective Cavanaugh said. "Well, I didn't point it out, at least not to too many people," Lynn said. Funny how our perceptions change when we really examine the facts, I thought.

When Detective Cavanaugh had finished asking questions and making notes on the art robbery, I told him what we'd seen at the old brewery building just an hour ago. We gave him the full story, including Norman, "the bruiser," the broken stair and the light.

Detective Cavanaugh shook his head and ran his fingers over his great moustache. "I want both of you to stay away from that brewery and particularly from Norman Trout!" he said emphatically.

"But you have to do something. I think he's selling drugs!" I stammered.

Cavanaugh looked from me to Lynne and back to me again. "I'm only telling you this because I've seen you go into action by yourself too many times, Karen. And I figure if I don't tell you you'll set up your own stakeout! So, you are now sworn to secrecy, both of you. You got that?"

I raised my right hand. "We swear. We won't tell a soul!" I said. Lynne raised her hand and said, "I promise, too."

"All right. Listen, I know Norman Trout is selling drugs. He's an undercover detective. He's with us! There's a meth dealer operating around here and that fellow you saw talking to Norman Trout is one of his hench men. We're setting up a sting to get to the head guy. And you two need to stay away from there!" Cavanaugh said.

"Wow! Norman Trout is an undercover cop! So what was he looking for going through Marvin's files?"

"Enough! Leave this to us, Karen. All right?"

What could I say? "Sure, sure," I said, nodding my head. "Could this tie in with Marvin's murder?" I asked.

"You mean the art theft?" Lynne asked, clearly focused on her loss.

"No, I mean the drug dealing," I said to Detective Cavanaugh.

"Karen, just leave this all to me this time, would you?"

"Of course," I said. Clearly, Detective Cavanaugh had shared all he was going to with me.

"I'll take those fingerprints and then I'm done here, Lynne. Just take a second look around and let me know if you see anything else out of place," Detective Cavanaugh said.

I accompanied Lynne as she walked gingerly through her own house. It had to be scary to know someone had been in your home when you weren't there. Nothing else seemed to be disturbed. Detective Cavanaugh finished dusting the front doorknob for fingerprints and left to interview the neighbors. Maybe they'd noticed someone coming to Lynne's while we were gone.

I stayed with Lynne a few minutes and then headed back home. I kept thinking about Marvin firing Norman. Had Marvin known that Norman was a cop? Probably not, or he wouldn't have fired him, right? And, what had Norman been looking for in Marvin's files?

These questions were rolling through my mind as I sped down Blackjack Road. I was coming up on Giroit Road and I hung a left. Giroit was a tiny road that wound around, and up and down, before coming out on Irish Hollow. Irish Hollow Road ran through the valley just about halfway between Blackjack Road and Highway 20. I followed Irish Hollow about a mile along the base of the valley. The fields here were planted in neat rows of corn. You rarely saw another person along here. In about five miles I came to the aptly named Devil's Ladder Road. This was a dirt road, just wide enough for a single vehicle. Three progressively steeper hills made seeing oncoming traffic impossible. And the shoulders were pretty much nonexistent. So if by chance you did meet another vehicle, you sat there, nose to nose, until one of you decided to back up to a widening somewhere to let the other pass. And, hopefully, you never ran into someone as you both crested the top of one of the hills! But this was the quickest way to get over to Highway 20 and I had an idea! It was time to visit Geri at Marvin's office. She'd worked as Marvin's receptionist and assistant for ten years. If anyone knew what Norman had been looking for, it would be Geri.

I made it up the 150 foot rise and drop on Devil's Ladder, twisted and turned around hairpin curves, saw the blueberry farm on my left where you could pick your own blueberries in a few weeks for a dollar a quart, and then came to Highway 20. Carl and Marvin's veterinary office was right there at the junction of Highway 20 and Devil's Ladder. I pulled into the small parking lot that Marvin had added when he'd purchased the old stone farmhouse that served as the clinic. A horse barn, riding ring, and a kennel flanked the clinic. As I walked up to the clinic door I was greeted by a chorus of barking. A large black Newfoundlander and a two Corgis Terriers pressed against the kennel's chain-link walls. No need for a doorbell here!

Geri sat behind an oak table that served as her desk. The living room of the old farmhouse had been converted into the reception room. Behind her, the kitchen served as the office/coffee room. Geri is tall, thin, tan and in her mid-thirties. Her desk held photos of her three children, two cats and a dog. With that size family I have no idea how she had time to stay in shape, or maybe that's what kept her in shape.

"Hi, Geri. How are you doing?" I asked. Her normal 1,000 watt smile was missing. She shrugged her shoulders in reply.

"I'm so sorry about Marvin," I said. It must be like losing a family member, I thought. They'd spent nearly every day together for the past ten years.

"Thanks. I don't know what we'll do without him around here," she said.

"I didn't know if you'd even be open today. I just took a chance and swung by."

A white and orange cat hopped up on the desk and sat next to Geri. She stroked its back absentmindedly and said, "Well, these guys have to be taken care of. And, we'll be closed tomorrow for Marvin's services. We're having a morning outdoor service at the Prospect

Cemetery on Rocky Hill Road. I hope you'll be able to come. We're inviting people to bring their pets, if they'd like to. It'll be a short service. Steven will play guitar and Carl will give the eulogy. That'll be it, really. Marvin wouldn't have wanted too much hoopla, as he would have called it."

"No church service?" I asked.

"No, Marvin wasn't a church-goer. He spent his time taking care of animals and hiking. So something outside will be fitting for him."

"What time did you say?"

"We're telling everyone to be there about 9 a.m. And please, let anyone know who you think would want to come. The paper doesn't come out until tomorrow afternoon, so it's just going to be word of mouth," Geri said.

"I will. In fact, that's sort of why I stopped here. You know I'm a friend of Ken's. And he and Marvin go way back."

"I know," she said.

"Well, Ken's as devastated about Marvin as you are," I said.

"I don't know what I'm going to do. I can't believe this happened on top of everything else this week," Geri said.

"Everything else? What do you mean?"

"My husband was laid off from work," Geri said.

"I'm so sorry. Where did he work?"

"At the Lesser Equipment factory," Geri said.

"Is that Roger Lesser's company?"

"Yes. I don't know what he'll do, now."

"Something will turn up," I assured her. "Geri, I know this is a terrible time for you but I'm trying to figure out what happened to Marvin. And, well, I was wondering if you could help me understand something," I said.

"Sure. If it'll help find out who killed Marvin, I'd do anything," Geri said and I could tell she meant it.

"Well, this may or may not have anything to do with Marvin's death, but it's been bothering me. Ken told me that Marvin fired Norman Trout because he'd caught Norman going through his files. Do you have any idea what Norman would have been looking for?"

"Yes, that was odd," Geri said tilting her head to the side and nodding. "But then, Norman was odd. There wasn't much in that cabinet Norman was going through. Most of our patient records are on computer now, you know. But we have some of our older files in the filing cabinet back there," Geri said, pointing toward the kitchen/office.

"Could there have been anything else in that filing cabinet?" I asked.

"Not much. We kept all the literature our suppliers sent us in there. You know the sort of thing: pamphlets on the latest pet medicines, special pet foods, flea and tick remedies. Oh, and Marvin kept some of his notes in there. He liked to keep track of his harder cases by hand. He'd keep a file on each animal, and write down things like what meds he'd used, what results, that sort of thing. He said it helped him to write things out."

"Was Marvin working on any cases like that now?" I asked.

"Well, there were some, sure. There pretty much always are some. Let's see, Mr. Heller's got an alpaca that's developed a limp. Alpaca are sort of new out here, so Marvin was doing some research on treating them. And, he'd been having a devil of a time with Brie's horse. That had been going on ever since she got it."

"Do you mean Elvis? I asked.

"No, this was her newest horse, Goldie. Between you and me, Marvin said that horse was really sick. He was trying to track down the owner and get its history, but he hadn't had any luck with that."

"I thought Brie's trainer had found the horse for her. Couldn't Marvin just ask him where he'd gotten it?"

"He had. But Harry just told Marvin the horse was in excellent condition when he'd bought it. Harry blamed Marvin for Goldie's condition. He claimed it was something Marvin had given the horse that made her lame."

"Do you think that could have been the case?" I asked.

"Well, it's not impossible, I suppose. I mean, Goldie could have been allergic to some medicine. But Marvin didn't think so."

Our conversation was drowned out as the barking chorus started again. A woman opened the front door and came in carrying a traveling case with a small dog peeking out of the cage. This was the most unusual dog I'd ever seen. It looked like a hairless dark brown Chihuahua except for a long tuft of white hair poking up on its small head. The little fellow was barking to beat the band, or maybe to beat the dogs outside!

"Hi, Marge!" Geri said to the woman. Seeing the little dog brought a smile to Geri's face that was nice to see. Life goes on. "Dr. Castoni is waiting for you. I'll let him know you're here," Geri said.

"And I'll let you get on with your work, Geri. Thanks for your help," I said. I had to stop to take a closer look at Marge's charge.

"He's a Chinese Crested," Marge said in reply to my unasked question. She must get that a lot.

"How unusual! Do you shave him?" I asked.

"No, that's their natural coat. They're great if you have allergies," she said with a laugh.

"I'll remember that," I said. The little dog gave a farewell yip and I headed out the door and back home.

I'd have to call Ken and let him know about tomorrow's funeral services for Marvin. Maybe he'd like to go together. Funerals are bad enough; it helps to go with a friend.

Chapter Twelve

Farewell, Marvin

It was 8:30 a.m. on Wednesday, and Ken stood in my doorway. He was here to pick me up for Marvin's funeral.

"Come on in," I said, opening the door. Then, glancing over his shoulder, I saw Baxter's giant head poking out of the window of Ken's truck. Baxter had the perfect English Mastiff face, black muzzle, tan coat and huge brown eyes. At a hundred and eighty-five pounds, Baxter was a force to be reckoned with. On cue, Baxter gave a bark that sent Truffs, who'd come to see who was at the door, scurrying up her living room cat-tree.

"Baxter is coming to the funeral service with us?" I asked.

"You said pets were invited, remember? And I expect there'll be a lot of dogs there. I haven't done much with Baxter lately, so I figured he'd enjoy the outing," Ken said.

"Sure," I said, wondering how Ken was going to keep Baxter under control when he saw the other dogs. Baxter was the biggest dog I'd ever seen and, thank heavens, he was also one of the nicest. Baxter and I had become great friends over the past few months as I'd gotten to know Ken. Truffs however, still had her reservations about the behemoth canine. I looked over at Truffs. Her ears had flattened back in preparation for combat. But she was safe where she was and I knew she'd go off "kitty-alert" when she heard us leave.

"I'll grab my purse and meet you in the truck," I said, dashing back to the kitchen table where I'd set my shoulder bag. I checked inside: cell phone, wallet, pen, mini notebook. Yep, it was all there.

I went over to Truffs and gave her a reassuring rub before I closed the front door behind me. Ken was waiting for me by his truck. I looked into his gorgeous blue eyes and met his smile. "Thank you, kind sir," I teased as Ken opened the passenger door for me. His gallantry was, in fact, quite charming. I took Ken's proffered hand and negotiated the step up as gracefully as I could. My daily exercise routine paid off here.

I settled myself in my seat as Ken closed the passenger door and then climbed into the driver's seat. Baxter was already greeting me with a large, pink-tongued lick.

"Down, boy! Baxter, down," Ken said. Baxter, tail thumping, lay down in the back seat with his head on the counsel between the two front seats.

"He's excited to see you," Ken said and then added, "We both are." Ken gave me a smile that warmed my heart.

"Good to see you, too," I said and smiled back. It really was good to be with him.

Ken swung the truck around my circular drive, past the rock garden where the yellow, orange and red daylilies formed a brilliant color display. Just looking at them made me want to paint them. Well, I'd be back in my studio tomorrow, I promised myself, and then turned my gaze and thoughts back to Ken.

"How are you doing?" Ken asked me.

"O.K., I guess. Still in a bit of shock, I think. First Marvin, then Brie, and then the art burglaries," I said. "I thought country life would be crime free after living in the city," I said.

"I know," Ken said. "Makes you feel very vulnerable, doesn't it?"

"Yes, I guess it does," I agreed. "But it also makes me want to know who's responsible," I said.

"You want to make your world safe again. You feel like you have to do everything you can to make it right—or as right as possible," he said.

"Exactly. I'm glad you understand," I said.

"And it means a lot to me. Thanks." We came to the top of my drive and Ken stopped the truck. He leaned over, looked into my eyes and gave me a kiss. Then he whispered in my ear, "I'm really glad we met."

"Me too," I whispered back.

He looked into my eyes again, patted my hand and then shifted his attention back to driving. We rode in silence heading to Prospect Cemetery.

It was another gorgeous July day. The sky was blue, the sun was warm. The trees were in full green glory. Blackjack is an old stagecoach route. It followed the ridge tops, twisting and turning, rising and falling, offering alternating farm, forest and prairie views. It made me conscious of being alive.

I looked out at the passing scenery. The corn fields were exceeding the expectations set by the old adage: "knee-high by the Fourth of July". Whether it was global warming or a natural cycle, we'd definitely had an early spring. The crops had a good start. I sure hoped they'd get the rain they needed to mature.

In these past few years of country living I've come to see how dependent farmers are on the variable and uncontrollable forces of nature. Too much rain and the crops rotted in the fields. Not enough and they withered. The farmers don't water the corn and soybean fields out here. Maybe it's too hilly to do that, I don't really know. In any event, the farmers here relied upon Mother Nature to water their fields.

And in just the past few years I'd seen both droughts and floods. Mother Nature seemed to be going through a change of life, complete with hot flashes and tumultuous storms. But this summer, things seemed perfectly in tune with growth. As a tourist I just saw the picturesque snap shot. Now, living out here, I see the fate of the local farmers in those knee high plants.

We rounded the corner at Batey Hollow and drove past the acres of wild flowers planted by our local nature club, the Natural Area Guardians. The prairie grasses were three feet tall now, half their full autumnal height. Heleopsis swayed in the gentle breeze, dotting the grasses with golden disks. There were hundreds of more delicate species of wild flowers and grasses tucked in there. I'd spent many an afternoon in my own fields and forests hiking with a guidebook in my hand, stooping to identify the greater lobelia, blue bell flowers, shooting stars, and the myriad of wild flowers in bloom.

Ten minutes later, we turned onto Rocky Hill Road and followed that for a mile or so to Cemetery Road. A young man waved us into the field designated for parking. Ken stopped the truck and walked around to open my door. I still wasn't accustomed to these old school manners but I knew I could get used to it. I took Ken's proffered hand and made the big step down from the truck.

There were already at least fifty cars and trucks here and more were pulling in behind us. Ken, Baxter and I walked across the lane to the cemetery. Prospect Cemetery is a small plot of land ringed by stately old oak trees. Glancing around, I noticed that the tombstones were all modest, grey granite. Many looked like they'd been there for a hundred years and I got the feeling you had to be an old-time country family to have a plot here. Marvin's family qualified, and he probably had ancestors laid to rest here. People stood talking in small, quiet groups; I saw several people I knew. Detective Cavanaugh was among them. I wondered if he was there under the assumption that Marvin's killer would attend the funeral. I'd seen Agatha Christie's detective, Hercule Poirot, do that in more than one mystery novel. I looked through the crowd with renewed interest.

Dara and Raymond Brown were there, as well as Carl and Clay Castoni and Polly Andrews. They were standing with a group I recognized from Galena Stables. Sassie and Ed Ballantine were talking to Brie's trainer, Harry Henry. This must be really hard for Captain Ed, I thought. Even though he couldn't have known Marvin's parachute was rigged to fail, it was still his hot air balloon that Marvin had jumped from. Tara Stone was seated in a chair at the edge of the small cemetery. A black hearse was parked behind her. There was a steady stream of people walking up to her giving her their condolences.

Baxter tugged at his leash as a couple with a small dog approached us. "Winston! Ken said. "Winston!" I echoed. A little pug came waddling up to us, obviously not intimidated in the least by Baxter's size.

"Hi, Fred," I said. "Let me introduce you to my friend, Ken. Fred and I met earlier this year when I came out to his farm to talk to his mother," I told Ken.

"Good to meet you," Fred said. Fred looked to be about the same age as Brie.

"This whole community is going to miss Marvin. Look around. Marvin took care of these folks' horses, cows, dogs and cats," Ken said.

"He took care of Winston here, and all our horses out at the farm. Carl is very good too, of course, but he's just starting out in his practice. He would have learned a lot from Marvin," Fred said.

My mind went to Brie's horse, Goldie. "Fred, were you and Brie friends? I mean, you look about the same age and you're both into horses. Did you know each other?"

"Yes, we were friends. We went to school together until she left and we reconnected when she moved back here," Fred said. "This has been incredible, both of them gone in the space of a few days," he said.

"Do you by any chance know anything about Brie's horses, Elvis and Goldie?" I asked.

"Sure, what do you want to know? We rode together all the time."

"Well, I've heard conflicting stories about Brie's new horse. Do you know how she came to buy it? Harry said he found it for her and it was in great shape when he bought it. In fact, Harry sort of blamed Marvin for Goldie's condition. She's lame, as I understand it."

"Yes, she is lame. But my own opinion is that Marvin had nothing to do with it. I saw that horse and it was showing signs of injury two days after Brie bought it. That was way before Marvin ever saw Goldie."

"Really! Then why was Harry blaming Marvin?" I asked.

"Why do you think? He'd bought a bad horse and Brie had paid top dollar for it. Harry wouldn't tell anyone where he bought the horse because he didn't want them checking into the horse's history, that's what I think!"

"What do you think about Brie's overdose?" Ken asked.

"I never saw Brie take any sort of drugs since she was back here," Fred said. "I know they say that's what killed her, but everything she said to me makes me think she had really kicked the drug habit."

"So you think someone might have injected her with the drugs?"

"I think that could have been it. I don't know why though, so I have to leave that to the police."

"Ken, I saw Detective Cavanaugh over there. I think we should mention this to him. Don't you?"

"Excuse us, Fred," I said, linking my hand in Ken's and leading him towards Detective Cavanaugh. Baxter and Winston gave each other a few farewell barks as we left.

We joined Detective Cavanaugh as he stood under a tree at the edge of the cemetery watching the group.

"Detective Cavanaugh, can we join you for a minute?" Ken asked.

Detective Cavanaugh folded his arms over his ample chest and nodded. He didn't seem all that pleased, but he gave us his attention.

"We were just was wondering if you'd heard anything more about Brie's death," I said.

"The autopsy confirmed death by an overdose injected into her arm," Detective Cavanaugh said.

"Have you talked to Fred Wood? He's a friend of Brie's and he's sure she did not use drugs anymore. Do you think someone else could have injected her?" I asked. "I guess I'm saying, with someone cutting Marvin's parachute rip cord, it could be that that same person killed Brie as well."

Detective Cavanaugh stared at me. "Thank you, Karen. Yes, we're looking into every possibility. And it would be better if you leave the investigation to me."

"Of course. I just wanted to let you know what people were telling us, that's all."

"Thank you for sharing that" Detective Cavanaugh said. We were clearly being dismissed. I looked from Detective Cavanaugh to Ken, nodded and walked away with Ken.

"Hmm. I think we should talk to Harry. If he sold Brie a sick horse, maybe she found out and he killed her to stop her from telling everyone. If his other clients knew that, he'd be out of business," I said.

"If he sold her a sick horse and killed her to keep her quiet, you'd better be careful," Ken said. "There've been two murders in this town already this week."

I could see he meant it. I let it drop—for now.

The crowd now gathered in a semicircle around Tara. She was seated next to Marvin's casket with Marvin's parents and his two brothers and their families seated next to her. The family faced the assembled crowd. Captain Ed and Sassie came and stood next to us under a large oak tree. The murmur of the crowd died away as Steven began playing a song on his guitar. When the music ended, Carl Castoni came forward and gave the eulogy. In fifteen minutes, the service was over. Marvin's father spoke for a minute and thanked everyone on behalf of the family and said they would hold the internment in private. And that was it.

We walked away in small groups. As we were leaving, Captain Ed asked Ken if we would join him and Sassie in a hot air balloon ride this evening in tribute to Marvin. It was a touching thought, and we said we would. We made plans to meet them at their place in the country at 6:00 p.m. then hugged our good-byes. Ken and I drove to my place in relative silence. The finality of Marvin's death was overwhelming.

Chapter Thirteen

Up, Up and Away

When Ken left, I sat alone on my screened in porch considering various scenarios. Ideas swirled through my mind and I realized I needed to write them down. I got out a set of index cards and spread them on the table in front of me. My plan was to write each suspect's name, motive and opportunity on an index card. I'd put any suspects in Marvin's death on the pile to my left and any suspects for Brie's murder in the pile to my right. Then I could cross match them. There had to be a connection between Brie's and Marvin's death.

So, first, who'd had anything in for Marvin? A few days ago I thought Norman was a prime suspect. But he's with the Sheriff's Department, so I crossed him off my mental list. I thought some more and wrote "Clay Castoni" on the top of one card and "Carl Castoni" on the top of the other. Under motives, I wrote: "advancing Carl's veterinary practice." Not a very good motive, but it was the best I could come up with. Opportunity—I suppose either of them could have been at Galena Stables early on Saturday. I'd have to check that out.

Captain Ed was the last person to see Marvin alive, so he had opportunity. But he was such a good guy, everyone in town loved him.

And that bogus motive about his being jealous of Marvin and Sassie had been dispelled by Ken. Captain Ed and Tara both knew that Sassie was just helping Marvin plan Tara's surprise birthday party.

There was Brie, of course, who is now dead. That didn't rule her out as Marvin's killer. I wrote Brie's name at the top of a card, entered: "anger over rejection" across from the word "motive" and "at stable" for opportunity.

Then there was Harry Henry. If he had a motive to kill Brie, maybe he had a motive to kill Marvin too that I just hadn't heard about yet. I wrote down Harry Henry's name on two index cards and put one on the table to my left and one on the table to my right. Harry would have had a motive if Marvin knew the horse Harry had sold Brie was sick. Maybe Marvin was getting tired of Harry's insinuations that Marvin had caused Goldie to go lame. Maybe Marvin had told Harry he was going to warn people that Harry had sold Brie a lame horse. That would have put Harry out of business, at least here in Galena. I wrote "stopping Marvin from telling people about Goldie" as a motive on Harry's card to my left.

Next, I turned my thoughts to Brie. If Brie had figured out that Harry knew Goldie was lame when he sold Brie the horse, that would have given Harry a motive to kill Brie to stop her from telling anyone else. I wrote that on Harry's card under: "motive." Harry had said that Brie had hired Norman because she blamed Marvin for injuring Goldie and felt badly that Marvin had fired Norman. But maybe Brie knew the truth about Norman. Maybe Brie had been working with Norman. The only one who could tell me that would be Norman himself, or maybe Detective Cavanaugh. I'd have to ask them about that when I got the chance.

Who else would have had a motive to kill Brie? I thought for a minute again. Brie was pretty well off. Her mother would inherit Brie's money, I suppose, since Brie was single and an only child. But Brie's mother was in New York and, well, she was Brie's mother! I didn't see Brie's mother as a suspect. Since I'd never heard anything about Brie's father, I thought it was safe to assume he was not a part of her life and not likely to inherit her estate. So, if he was alive, he probably did not have a motive.

Carl and Clay didn't seem to have any strong connection to Brie, so I didn't see either of them as suspects in her death.

Which brought me back to Brie herself. She was obsessed with Marvin. That seemed to be general knowledge. She could have been so upset with his death that she took her own life. Or, she could have killed Marvin and then killed herself out of remorse. Much as I disliked that scenario, it was possible. I filled out a card for Brie as suspect in her own death.

There were other people I didn't really know at Galena Stables. Roger Lesser kept several horses at the stable. And he and Henry had been arguing about something the other night at the winery event. But he seemed to be a successful businessman and involved in the community. He seemed an unlikely suspect, but for lack of any other names, I wrote his name down but left motive blank. He'd been at the Fourth of July Horse Show at Galena Stables. He could have been there early when Marvin had done his rounds. That would have given Roger opportunity. I'd have to check that out. I made a card out for him as a suspect in Brie's murder as well. But I drew a blank when it came to motive. He certainly could have been at the stables the morning Brie had been killed. Galena Stables is pretty much open to whoever drives in. So that means anyone without a specific alibi could have had opportunity. Yikes. This wasn't going to be easy!

I looked at my watch and it was already noon. Ken was coming back to get me about 5:30 p.m. for our balloon ride. That gave me a few hours to look at my painting again and still have time to pack for tomorrow's trip to Asheville. So that's just what I did. The afternoon flew by. Before I knew it, I was standing in front of my closet with Truffs in my arms. She was helping me decide what to wear for a hot air balloon ride. I pulled out jeans, a long-sleeved, white, lycra shirt and my running shoes. I didn't know much about hot air balloons I figured I should be in my most comfortable active wear.

Ken picked me up right on time and we headed out towards Eagle Ridge Resort. Captain Ed and Sassie lived just outside the Galena Territory, fairly close to Galena Stables. They had their own five hundred acre tract of land and Captain Ed ran his hot air balloon excursions out of a steel pole barn on their property. We drove up to the barn and found Captain Ed, Sassy and a crew of four young people preparing the hot air balloon for our trip. They had the red, yellow and orange striped balloon spread out flat on the ground. The basket that we would be riding in lay on its side at the base of the balloon. A giant fan had been placed at the base of the balloon.

"Hey, Karen and Ken. Glad you're going to join us for this ride. Marvin would like that. And sunset's a gorgeous time to fly in a balloon," Captain Ed said. Sassy came over and gave Ken and me a hug hello.

"I'm looking forward to this. It's my first balloon ride," I said, somewhat sheepishly. I was both excited and a little bit afraid. How was he going to steer this thing? And hot air balloons have a giant torch right in the balloon to heat the air so they'll rise. Was it really a good idea to go up in a giant nylon balloon with a torch in the center of it? I felt my heart race and asked Captain Ed as casually as I could, "How often do you go up in this balloon?"

"You're nervous! That's natural on your first ride. I've been flying this balloon for ten years now and I've never had an accident. We'll be just fine. The winds are at less than five miles an hour on the ground and that's just what we want. That's why we take off early in the morning or late in the day when the winds die down as the land cools.

"Oh," I said. "That's good."

"Let me tell you a little about the balloon. Maybe that'll make you more comfortable. Once we have the balloon filled, it'll be holding 240,000 cubic feet of air. There's a propane burner in the center of the basket that'll throw off 15 million Btu's. In comparison, your home furnace has about 15 thousand Btu's."

Knowing I was riding with millions more Btu's next to me wasn't exactly making me feel more comfortable. I swallowed hard.

"It'll be one of the best experiences of your life. Trust me," Captain Ed said.

I guess I was going to.

"Hit it!" Captain Ed yelled to one of the young men. Suddenly a giant fan started blowing air into the balloon and conversation became impossible. Ken and I stepped back to get away from the blast of air and the noise. It took about fifteen minutes for the balloon to fill but it still looked a bit limp. That's when Captain Ed hit the burner. Flame shot into the center of the balloon and it began to rise. As the balloon lifted the basket began to tip upright. "Climb into the gondola!" Captain Ed yelled. One of the young men placed a stepping stool next to the basket and Captain Ed hopped in first. Sassie quickly climbed in right behind him. I studied her moves. There didn't seem to be any particularly graceful way to do this. I looked back at Ken who nodded to me. I climbed the three steps then braced my hands on the side of the woven basket and swung myself over the side and in. My feet landed on the plywood base of the basket with a thump but that was drowned out by the explosive sound of the burner. I moved aside quickly and Ken heaved himself over the side and into the basket. There were two ropes tied to the sides of the basket and two of the ground crew held the lines. When Captain Ed pulled on a silver handle just to the right of his head, a blast of propane flame exploded up into the balloon and the balloon lifted ever so slightly off the ground and then settled again. Captain Ed nodded to the crew and they untied the tethering ropes from the basket. Captain Ed blasted the gas again and the flame roared up not three feet from my head. I looked up into the center of the balloon.

Captain Ed followed my gaze and explained: "The colored part of the balloon is called the envelope. That's the part that holds the air. The uppermost part is called the crown. The rope you see attached to the crown and the gondola is the crown line. That aligns the envelope with the gondola. The opening at the bottom of the envelope is called the mouth. This is the balloon's rip cord." Captain Ed said pointing to a rope hanging near his head. "If I pull that, it'll open the rip panel at the top of the crown and let air out. There are also flaps on this side of the envelope called maneuvering vents that I can open to release air a little at a time," Captain Ed said. "And this is the burner. Look here," he said, pointing to a series of gauges next to him. "This is the altimeter that tells me how high we are above the ground. This is the balloon calculator that tells how fast the balloon is flying. I have a compass here to tell the direction of our flight. The fuel gauge tells how much fuel we have left. The pyrometer tells me the temperature of the air inside the envelope and the variometer tells me the feet per minute the balloon is rising or falling. This is the burner" Captain Ed said pointing to a metal canister located just above our heads. He gave a metal handle at shoulder height a tug and flames shot up again into the center of the balloon.

"All set?" Captain Ed asked looking at Ken and me.

We nodded and Captain Ed fired the burner even longer this time. We began to hover and then moved, much more slowly than I expected, toward the edge of the mowed field. Rows of corn loomed ahead at the height of our basket. I looked over the edge and wondered if we were going to be able to get up into the air all right. The corn fields were edged with trees. If we drifted over the corn fields at this height we might wreck the crop. But if we weren't a lot higher than this by the time we got to the end of the field, we'd crash into the trees! And what would happen to that giant inferno in the center of this thing!

Captain Ed gave the burner another burst of gas. There was now a steady flame rising into the center of the balloon. This was it. It looked like he had that burner fully open. Just at the edge of the grass field the balloon lifted and we tickled the tops of the corn with the bottom of the basket. Then we began to rise in earnest. By the time we were at the end of the corn field we were just higher than the tops of the trees. Soon I was looking down at the birds. Captain Ed turned off the burner and we floated in complete silence. "This is what you call free flight," Captain Ed said. The scenery was breathtaking in 360 degree panoramic view. I completely forgot my nervous fear. I leaned over the edge of the basket and took in the sights. Bright green fields of corn alternated with dark green, tree-covered hills. Three deer ran along the edge of the field below us and scampered into the woods. Every now and then we saw a farm house nestled in the valley. It looked like a model with tiny electrical wires running to it and a tiny truck parked in the gravel drive.

"I can control our elevation with this burner" Captain Ed told us. He put his hand on the silver lever, pulled down and a burst of flame shot into the air.

"But the wind controls our direction. Right now we're flying back toward the river. We'll just drift along up here and when we're ready to set down you can help me scout a good site."

"What's a good site?" I asked.

"We don't want any electrical wires, for instance," Captain Ed said. And we want road access nearby so the chase truck can get to us."

"The chase truck?" I asked.

"That's how we'll get back. Like I said, I can't steer this balloon. I can only control when we go up and down. So, see that truck down there? They're following us. That's our chase truck and they'll pick us up when we land."

I nodded. Sounded like a plan. Ken took my hand in his and gave me a squeeze.

Looking down I saw a hawk circle below us riding the currents just the way we were. This really was fun. "Let's go look at that farm house," Captain Ed said. We drifted along in silence without the roar of the burner and slowly settled lower. We were probably about a hundred feet in the air. The house was located at the top of a hillside. It was built of white wood and several tall pine trees stood alongside the house. A small garden had been planted out back. As our balloon drifted along, a family cemetery came into view. It made me think of time passing by so quickly—and of Marvin.

Captain Ed must have been thinking of Marvin too because he said, "I can't believe he's gone."

"I know," Ken said. "Me either."

"You were the last one to talk with him," Ken said to Captain Ed. "Did he say anything that might give us a clue about who's responsible?"

Captain Ed looked at Sassy and then back to Ken and me. "Well, I don't suppose there's any harm in my telling you. I already told Detective Cavanaugh when he interviewed me."

"Told him what?" I asked, probably sounding too eager because Ken squeezed my hand again.

Captain Ed hesitated and then said, "Ken, I know how close you and Marvin were, so that's why I'm telling you this. Marvin said he'd tried to call Detective Cavanaugh just before we took off. He said he hoped Detective Cavanaugh didn't call while he was doing the jump because he really wanted to talk to him and he didn't want to miss the call."

"Did Marvin say why he'd called Detective Cavanaugh?" Ken asked.

"He said he had to tell him about what he'd overheard in the stable before the show. He didn't say what he'd heard or who he'd heard. Just that he had to let Detective Cavanaugh know."

"Oh, I sure wish he'd told you what he wanted to tell Detective Cavanaugh. If he had, I think that we'd know who killed Marvin," Ken said.

"I know. I've been thinking the same thing. And I've racked my brain, but Marvin didn't say anything else to me about it. And I was too focused on the flight to press him about it."

We drifted on in silence again, lost in our own thoughts. As we crested a ridge, Highway 20 came into view. "We must be drifting southwest," I said. "Maybe we'll fly over my place and we can land there! How much fun would that be!" I said.

"Maybe," Captain Ed said. But I think we're going to be too far west to hit your place. I'd like to land on this side of the Mississippi, though. There's a lot of open land off Irish Hollow Road. Maybe we'll land by the Norwegian Fiord horses and the fallow deer!" I said.

"I try not to land close to cows or horses or any farm animals. The balloon scares them. So we'll look for an open field that hasn't been planted this year," Captain Ed said.

"Are there many of those?" I asked.

"Sure. There's lots of CRP acreage out here," Captain Ed said. "If I land in someone's corn or soybeans I have to buy the crop I damage and the farmers don't like it. Neither do I. But the CRP is a federal Conservation program that pays farmers to take their highly erodible fields out of production to build up the soil bank. So it doesn't hurt anything if I land there."

"Building up the soil bank is an excellent idea. I know my fields were planted in corn before I bought the property and in some places the soil was only a few inches deep. Then you hit rock!"

"Exactly. So the Conservation Reserve Program fields will look like tall grass fields and that's a great place to land," Captain Ed said. "Help me look."

We all leaned over the side of the basket and looked for open fields without power lines. We'd been up about an hour now and as we came over the ridge that bordered Highway 20, Irish Hollow valley opened up below us. It was gorgeous and Ken pointed to a flat open area about a mile ahead.

"That looks good," Captain Ed said and pulled the rip cord hanging next to him. Air rushed out of the top of the balloon and we slowly but steadily lost altitude.

In a few more minutes we were brushing along the top of the grasses and then the gondola bumped onto the ground. I held onto the side of the basket and widened my stance to steady myself. Our basket took a few hops along the ground. Captain Ed let more air out of the balloon and the basket stopped and steadied itself. The chase truck came around the bend and pulled up to the edge of the field. Three of the guys ran out and attached ropes to the basket. The balloon had landed.

I looked around wondering about how I'd exit this basket. The walls of the basket were about chest high. Captain Ed must have read my body language because he said, "Don't worry about getting out yet. The guys will walk the balloon back over to the truck so we don't have to carry it. This thing weights two thousand pounds so you don't want to have to move it very far!"

"Really!" I said. I hadn't expected a balloon to be so heavy. Captain Ed gave the balloon a bit of gas, just enough to lift the balloon a foot off the ground. The three guys reattached ropes to the basket and led the balloon back to the edge of the field near the truck.

Once we were there, Ken easily hoisted himself over the side and then lifted me by my waist and helped me hop out. Captain Ed and Sassy climbed out easily, they'd obviously had lots of practice at this. Then Captain Ed pulled the rip cord and the balloon completely deflated. The ground crew folded and stowed the balloon, ropes and basket onto a trailer in back of the chase truck, Captain Ed retrieved a bottle of champagne out of a cooler in the back of the truck. Sassy grabbed four silver glasses and a box of chocolates and handed us each a glass and several pieces of gold foil wrapped chocolate.

"What's this?" I asked in surprise.

"This is an old balloonists' tradition," Captain Ed said. "Whenever we land, we have a toast of champagne and chocolates and I tell any new balloonists the history of hot air balloons."

"Wonderful!" I exclaimed.

"Let's have a toast!" Captain Ed said. He popped the champagne cork and poured each of us a glass. "Raise your glasses," Captain Ed said and then recited this verse:

The winds have welcomed you with softness,

the sun has blessed you with its warm hands

You have flown so high, and so well,

that God has joined you in your laughter

and set you gently back again into the

loving arms of Mother Earth.

We each drank to the experience. "Karen and Ken, you are now officially aeronauts!"

Then Captain Ed said, "And raise your glass again, to our dear friend, Marvin."

"To Marvin," we echoed.

As we finished our champagne, Captain Ed gave us the brief version of hot air balloon history.

"The first hot air balloon called 'Aerostat Reveillon' was launched in September of 1783 by Pilatre De Rozier. The passengers were a sheep, a duck and a rooster and the balloon flew for a total of fifteen minutes. A few months later, two French brothers, Joseph and Etienne Montgolfier launched their balloon from the center of Paris and flew twenty minutes. That was the first manned balloon flight and it is heralded as the birth of hot air ballooning. Two years later, a French balloonist, Jen Pierre Blanchard, and the American co-pilot, John Jefferies, were the first to fly across the English Channel. That same year, De Rozier attempted to cross the English Channel with a hydrogen balloon and a hot air balloon tied together. Unfortunately, the balloon exploded and Rozier was killed.

"In 1793 Jen Pierre Blanchard flew the first hot air balloon in North America. George Washington was there to watch the launch. It took over a hundred years for hot air balloons to reach the stratosphere. In 1932 Swiss scientist Auguste Piccard reached 52,498 feet setting a new altitude record. Balloonists continued to set new altitude records for the next few years. In 1935 Explorer 2 set the record at 72,395 feet and held the record for twenty years. They proved that humans could survive that altitude in a pressurized chamber and paved the way for the future of air travel.

"In 1978 the Double Eagle II became the first balloon to cross the Atlantic. That was a helium balloon carrying three passengers: Ben Abruzzo, Maxie Anderson and Larry Newman. The flight took one hundred and thirty-seven hours. In 1981 the Double Eagle V flew across the Pacific in an eighty-four hour flight.

"In 1987 Richard Branson and Per Lindstrand were the first to fly across the Atlantic in a hot air balloon rather than a helium gas balloon. They did it in thirty-three hours, breaking another record. They flew again in 1991 and were the first to cross the Pacific in a hot air balloon.

Finally, in 1999 the first around the world flight was completed by Bertrand Piccard and Brian Jones. They flew for almost twenty days launching from Switzerland and landing in Africa.

And today, you joined the lucky few who can call themselves aeronauts! Congratulations!" Captain Ed concluded.

We all four raised our glasses in one final toast, "To new adventures," I said.

"To new adventures," Ken, Captain Ed and Sassie said in unison.

Chapter Fourteen

Jet Set

Thursday morning at 8:00 a.m., I hugged Louise and Tony, petted Truffs and headed out to my neighbor's airstrip. Burt Castle was a retired United Airlines pilot who had started a small chartering business to help defray expenses on his twin engine, Cessna 303 Crusader. Burt had a grass airstrip just a few miles from me off Batey Hollow Road. I'd chartered Burt and his plane to fly me to Asheville. Yes, chartering a plane was an extravagance. But I had won the lottery. And even the interest on the principal of my winnings was a chunk of change. I figured I needed to spend some of it, just to help the local economy, if nothing else.

My personal acquisition habits were, quite frankly, abysmal. I mostly just painted. And you really can't spend much doing that. On top of which, because Marshall was able to sell my paintings in his New York Gallery, I actually made money with my paintings. Go figure! True, I did indulge in a few designer outfits on my occasional trips into Chicago. But for the most part, I wore jeans and tennies. I was definitely now more of a country girl than the city lawyer I once was.

Burt appreciated my business and he was an excellent pilot. Given the hassles of today's airports: the hours of driving to the airport, the parking, removing my shoes, luggage searches, and transferring any liquids I wanted to carry on the plane into four ounce bottles, I considered chartering Burt's plane a wonderful indulgence. And Burt had agreed to fly me to Asheville on just a week's notice.

I took a left off Batey Hollow Road and drove down through the metal gate. A gravel road ran parallel to the grass runway. The runway was located on the leveled hilltop and followed that ridge about a mile. Lights were mounted in the ground every fifty yards or so along the edge of the grass strip. They were turned off now, but I knew from our last trip that Burt could illuminate those runway lights with a flick of a switch right from the plane's cockpit. At the end of the runway stood a large metal building that served as the airplane's hanger. This was exciting and the adrenaline in my body brought everything into sharp focus. Two flights in two days from right here in the country. Life was good. Enjoy it while we have it, right?

I pulled the Boxster into the air hanger and put its convertible top up against exploring raccoons, mice and other country creatures. Burt was waiting for me, doing his preflight check on the plane.

"Good morning, Karen. You're right on time," Burt said, checking his watch.

"I try to be. I really appreciate your flying me this morning."

"No problem. I'm glad to do it. Since I retired, I appreciate every opportunity to get up in the sky—especially when you're buying the gas!" Burt said with a smile. "Let me just finish going over my checklist here," Burt said.

"Take all the time you need. Don't let me rush you," I said, and really meant that. Truth be told, I was a nervous flyer even though I found it exciting as well. I knew the statistics were that I was safer flying than driving, but I had to keep telling myself that. I traveled with a small box of Galena Chocolates—my preferred method of self medication. I patted my purse just to make sure they were there.

"All set!" Burt said. "Do you have any luggage?" he asked looking around for my suitcase.

"In the boot!" I said. Burt walked to the front of the Boxster and opened the front hood. The Boxster has two trunks to make up for the tiny space of each compartment.

"Is that it?" Burt asked, lifting my leather suitcase and shoulder bag.

"Yup," I said. "That's it. I travel light." I closed the Boxster's hood pressing it down to make sure it was fully closed and then pressed the lock button on my key. The Boxster flashed its lights at me in acknowledgment that it was indeed securely locked until my return.

"All in then," Burt said and we climbed into the airplane. The Cessna seated six people and had retractable gear. That was all I knew about the plane even though I sat in the co-pilot's seat. I'd watched Burt closely whenever I'd flown with him, but I sure hoped I'd never have to try to fly this plane.

Burt sat in the pilot's seat and put on his headset and microphone. He proceeded with his in-plane checklist and started up the engines. "She's ready to fly," Burt said. "Are you?"

"Ready!" I said, grabbing the arm rests and thinking about reaching in my purse for a chocolate.

We taxied onto the runway and then Burt gave the engines full throttle. We rolled along the bouncy grassy strip and then magically rose into the air. Flying over Blackjack Road, the trees and hills shrunk as my aerial perspective broadened with our ascent. Now this was getting to be fun. I looked for my place and its attached silo but we were already over Galena. I felt the plane's wheels retract and tuck into the belly of the airplane.

"Wow! You really move out in this plane!" I said.

"Yup. We're doing 178 knots. That's 205 miles per hour. We should be in Asheville about 11:30 a.m. It's just about a three hour flight," Burt said. "So relax. Make yourself comfortable."

I reached into my purse for a chocolate.

Burt talked to control towers as we passed above Springfield, Illinois. I thought of how different this flight was than yesterday's hot air balloon ride. The airplane's engines gave off a steady drone. Yesterday's flight had been most memorable in the moments of completely silent drifting. The dials and gauges were much more complex here and spread across the front of the plane. There was a set for the nonexistent co-pilot as well. And looking down, we were so much higher that the world below us seemed much more removed.

Between chatting with Burt about his other recent trips and watching the scenery change, the three hour flight passed quickly. Asheville's air control tower cleared us for landing at 11:20 a.m. Burt parked the Cessna and said he planned to grab a bite of lunch and then head back. I'd arranged to rent a car at the airport and one of the fellows at the general aviation hanger gave me a lift over to the car rental lot. As the clerk at the car rental agency did the paperwork, I studied the directions to my hotel that I'd printed out on Map Quest last night. Thankfully, the hotel wasn't far. By noon I was on the road.

I was really looking forward to seeing the Biltmore. It was America's largest home and its acres of gardens are supposed to be spectacular. I was getting excited already. In less than a half hour, I turned onto the tree lined entrance road and drove through the tall, brown brick gates. This was it, the legendary Biltmore Estate.

I'd done a little research on the computer last night and learned that the Biltmore House had been constructed by George Vanderbilt, heir to the fortune created by American industrialists Cornelius Vanderbilt and William Henry Vanderbilt. The house was started in 1889 and completed six years later. The house features four acres of floor space, two hundred and fifty rooms, thirty-four bedrooms, forty-three bathrooms, and sixty-five fireplaces. The basement has a swimming pool, gymnasium, bowling alley and kitchens. The grounds are just as incredible. They include one hundred and twenty-five thousand acres, which landscape architect Frederick Law Olmsted, who created New York's Central Park, developed into acres of gardens, parkland and the first managed forest in America. The French Broad River flowed thorough the valley at the edge of the property. The family has opened the estate to the public including a working farm, a botanical garden, a conservatory, two restaurants and a winery. I drove down the twisting two lane road for about five miles before coming to the grey stone hotel built to accommodate overnight tourists. Although relatively new, the hotel was marked by old world service and luxury. I pulled into the circular drive and a valet opened my car door for me. From that point on, everything was taken care of for me. A uniformed young man guided me to the registration desk and said my bags would be waiting for me in my room when I got there. And so they were.

My room was actually a suite and it was gorgeous. Decorated in a yellow and white motif with blue accents, it was cheerful as well as tasteful. The leaded glass windows looked out at the dense surrounding forest. I unpacked and checked my cell phone in case I'd missed hearing a call from Ken or Detective Cavanaugh. No luck. Neither had called.

Hmm…What's a girl to do? Just then, there was a knock on my door. Who in the world could that be, I wondered. I looked through the tiny peephole and saw Bella smiling back at me.

"Bella!" I said, opening the door wide to let her enter.

Bella gave me a hug and said, "I'm your welcoming committee! I asked the desk to let me know when you arrived. This place is gorgeous and I've been waiting to tour the house until you got here!"

"Excellent! I was just wondering what I'd do this afternoon.

"Well, I have to be back at the horse show to oversee preparations for tomorrow's Grand Prix Dinner, but that's not until 3:00 this afternoon. So we have two hours to tour together."

I called the desk and was told that shuttle service to the main house was available. No need to get my car. Great! I wouldn't have to hassle with driving or directions.

When we got to the lobby a black limousine awaited us outside. I guess there's shuttle service and then there's Shuttle Service. The uniformed driver opened the door and Bella and I slid in onto the soft black leather seat.

"Welcome to the Biltmore, ladies. My name is James," the middle aged man said.

"Thank you, James," I said. "This is our first visit to the Biltmore. We hear the house is an incredible sight. That's where we'd like to go," I said.

"You'll want to tour the house, of course, but don't forget to see the gardens. They are extraordinary," James said.

"I might just do that later this afternoon. We'll be here all weekend for the Biltmore Summer Classic Horse Show," I said.

"Excellent, Madame," James said as he pulled away from the hotel and continued on the two lane road I'd driven up when I arrived. "The gardens are behind the main house. I'll take you up to the main entrance and you'll be able to start your house tour there," James said.

"That sounds perfect," Bella said.

James drove down the tree lined road at a leisurely pace which seemed to fit the surroundings. The drive up to the Biltmore House was designed to impress—and it succeeded. A mile long driveway led up to the four story stone mansion. I had never seen a house like it. And I don't think another one exists! A grass esplanade with fountains, reflecting pools and statuary created a sort of park in the front yard. The drive up to the house went along the right side of this park-like area and then circled in front of the house and made a return drive down the left side. This was one of America's castles and I couldn't wait to see what was inside.

The house is built of large blocks of grey stone with dark trim around the windows. And with two hundred and fifty rooms, this house has a lot of windows. I counted ninety across the front alone! Four tower-like structures punctuating the long expanse of house added to the impression of a castle. The main entrance brought us into a wood paneled hall.

A smiling young woman greeted us and invited us to join the group that had just started its tour. She gave us headphones so we could listen to the recorded audio tour and then sent us on to the group of twenty folks ahead of us. The tour group had stopped just off the long wood paneled entrance hall in the glass enclosed Winter Garden. Lush ferns, extravagant orchids and a collection of other plants graced this indoor garden. "Mr. Vanderbilt had a great interest in horticulture as you will see in the gardens and greenhouses," our tour guide said. "Plants would be brought into bloom in the greenhouses and then moved here for the Vanderbilts' and their guests' enjoyment."

The first floor turned out to be the public entertaining area of the home. From the Winter Garden, we entered the dark wood paneled billiard room. The rich dark colors and leather chairs gave it a manly-man feeling. The billiard room adjoined the formal banquet hall. The hall was two stories high and contained a dark wooden table running the length of the room. Tall carved chairs gave the feeling of being ready to host a royal feast. Beautiful paintings and sculptures lined the walls. From this room we moved on to the adjoining breakfast room, a salon with a spectacular print collection, a music room with an extensive adjoining loggia, and the tapestry gallery featuring the Vanderbilt family portraits. The library was located just off the tapestry gallery and featured a stunning hand painted ceiling. And this was just the first of four floors, I thought in astonishment. The craftsmanship that went into this house reminded me of the palaces I had seen in Florence. I suppose this was the same thing in a way, the wealthiest individuals creating the best possible home.

Our guide pointed out that Mr. Vanderbilt had been at the leading edge of technology at the time. The home was wired for electricity, one of the first.

From the first floor we climbed the duly named Grand Staircase. As our guide told us, this spiral stone staircase, has one hundred and two stairs leading all the way to the fourth floor. Suspended from a single point in the center of the staircase, hangs an iron chandelier containing seventy-two electric light bulbs. We entered the second floor and walked into another long, wood-paneled living hall filled with comfortable furniture arranged in multiple seating groups. "This is where the family and guests would have visited and played card games," our guide told us. I imagined a festive gathering with guests decked out in their finery, laughing, and chatting. The tour continued along the second floor to Mr. Vanderbilt's bedroom and his adjoining Oak Sitting Room which featured a view of his land and his bronze sculpture collection. Mrs. Vanderbilt's ornate oval bedroom adjoined the other end of the Oak Sitting Room. There were other rooms on this second floor but our tour continued up the stairs to the third floor. There we toured the Raphael Room and the Earlom Room, both named for the paintings they showcased; and the South and North Tower Rooms, named for their locations and spectacular views. These rooms were extraordinarily appointed guest rooms. Staying here must have been quite an experience.

Now we ascended to the very tip-top of the mansion. The stairs narrowed as we climbed to the fourth floor to see the servants' bedrooms, baths, and servants' living hall. As you might guess, the rooms were on a much simpler and smaller scale here.

At this point, the tour descended all four flights to the Vanderbilt's exercise facilities. This was a gymnasium, swimming pool, bowling alley and changing rooms. It was a veritable health club. The basement also contained the inner workings of the house. There were three rooms dedicated to nothing but laundry. There was one room dedicated to the motor for the grand organ in the music room. And last but not least, there were nine rooms dedicated to kitchen facilities including: a vegetable pantry, a walk-in refrigerator, a pastry kitchen, a rotisserie kitchen, a main kitchen, a kitchen pantry just for gadgets, a canning pantry and another small pantry. Clearly eating well had been a high priority for the Vanderbilts and their guests. This was the highlight of the tour for Bella. Our tour guide explained that one of Mr. Vanderbilt's goals was to make Biltmore House entirely self-sustaining. To that end, he had extensive vegetable and herb gardens planted as well as a fruit orchard and a vineyard. Biltmore Estate follows his plan to this day and even raises its own beef and dairy cattle used in the Biltmore's two restaurants.

"The winery is open for complimentary wine tastings, cooking demonstrations and seminars," our guide told us at the conclusion of our tour.

"We'll have to tour the winery!" Bella said. Then she looked at her watch and added, "Later. I've got to run! I'm meeting the Biltmore's head of catering in fifteen minutes to talk about arrangements for the Grand Prix dinner."

I left Bella at the mansion's back entrance and sat down on a bench behind the house for a rest. I looked out at an incredible expanse of gardens sweeping down the hillside from the house. What a view! Long grass walkways lined with acres of flowers led to an extensive rose garden. The enclosed greenhouse stood just beyond the outdoor gardens at the base of the hill.

I figured I'd rest here and make a few calls, then continue my tour. I flipped open my cell and saw that I had messages from both Ken and Dara. I called Ken first.

Just hearing his hello made me smile. "Ken, it's me," I said.

"Hi! So you made it to Asheville all right?" Ken asked.

"Safe and sound. I'm meeting Tissy here tonight for dinner, and I just finished an incredible tour of the Biltmore House with Bella. I wish you could be here to see this place," I said.

Baxter barked in the background. "I just don't feel like a party right now. I hope you understand," Ken said.

"Oh, I do. Not a problem. I just think sometime you'd enjoy seeing this place," I said.

"I stopped in the clinic to talk to Carl this morning," Ken said. "Remember that little snippet I heard at the winery about a woman from Asheville e-mailing him looking for her horse?" Ken asked me.

"Oh, right. We never did learn her name," I said.

"Well, I just did," Ken said. "I mentioned to Carl that you were in Ashville and suggested that you could call her while you were there," Ken said. "So Carl went into his computer and printed out the old e-mail for me. When I got home I called her. Her name is Cheryl Cushing and I have a phone and address for you as well. If you talk to her could you find out who sold her horse for her? Maybe we could find her horse for her when you're back here," Ken said.

"Do you think this is connected with Marvin's murder?" I asked.

"I don't know. It's a loose end. And I'd like to get back to her for Marvin. She reached out to him for help and if we can help her, I'd like to do that," Ken said.

"I'll give Cheryl Cushing a call," I said.

"Why don't you see if you can get together with her? Sometimes you can learn a lot more talking in person than on the phone," Ken said.

"Hmm. O. K. I guess that's true," I said.

"When I talked to Cheryl I gathered that she's an older woman who loves horses. She sounded very pleasant. Even so, maybe you'd better take someone with you just to be safe," Ken said.

"I'll see what I can do. Maybe Bella or Tissy will be able to join me," I said. "What's the news on those two art thefts?" I asked.

"Well, the paper doesn't come out until next week, so I haven't read anything about them. I guess you'd have to call Lynne Shaw or Liz Seelig and see what they've heard. You could call Detective Cavanaugh, but I don't think he'll be very talkative," Ken said.

"I'll give him a call. Maybe he'll talk to me, given our history on those two other cases," I said.

"Or not," Ken said, with a laugh. Ken was right. Detective Cavanaugh wouldn't be happy to hear I was acting as an unofficial detective. He liked to work alone. Oh well. It couldn't hurt to give him a call.

"I'm about to tour the gardens here," I said to Ken. "I have a message from Dara, so I'll call her back, and then take a walk. I'll send you a picture of the mansion on my phone," I said.

"I'll look for it," Ken said. "Take care of yourself down there."

"I will. And I'll let you know when I talk to Cheryl," I added.

"Thanks," Ken said and we hung up.

I dialed Dara's number and got her at home. "Dara, it's Karen. I see you called my cell. Are you in Galena or are you down here in Asheville?" I asked.

"I'm driving to Asheville now. I'm just about two hours away. I want to be there for the Grand Prix tomorrow night," she said.

"It sounds like that's going to be quite an event!" I said. Tissy was telling me there's a $25,000 purse. That should make it exciting," I said.

"It will! Let's sit together at the dinner," Dara suggested.

"Great. Hey, Dara, have you by any chance heard anything about Detective Cavanaugh's progress?"

"You mean about Marvin and Brie or the art thefts?" Dara asked.

"Both," I said.

"Well, I haven't heard anything new about the murders but I did hear that Detective Cavanaugh is convinced the art thefts were by someone local," Dara said.

"Right. Because no one else would know about the Heade. But what about the Caitlin? How many people in town do you think knew the value of that painting?" I asked.

"Not many. The people on the Galena Art Museum Board probably knew it was valuable, but I just don't think they'd be art thieves. I don't see how someone local could sell these paintings. There's just not that kind of art market here," Dara said.

"They could take them to Chicago or maybe out West. Santa Fe has an incredible art market. Paintings sell there for tens and even hundreds of thousands of dollars," I said. "But a reputable dealer wouldn't just buy art like that without knowing where it came from.

They'd want to have the provenance of the painting when they're spending that kind of money," I said.

"Well, let's look at it another way. Who in Galena would know about the artwork and have a need for the money?" Dara asked me.

"You'd have a better idea of that than me. You know the people in town," I replied.

"Let me think about that one. I'll make a few calls and let you know what I hear," Dara said.

"Thanks. Well, drive safely and I'll see you at the horse show tomorrow. I'm staying at the Biltmore Inn so you can call me there on my cell if you hear anything," I said.

"I'm staying there too," Dara said. "So maybe I'll see you tonight.

"Excellent," I said and rang off.

I made one more call before I headed out on my garden tour. I reached Cheryl Cushing and made arrangements to meet her at her home tomorrow morning at 10:00 a.m. She was excited to learn that I was from Galena and that I was here at the horse show. I guess she figured that meant I could help her track down her horse. Her faith on that point was stronger than mine but I figured I'd talk to her since I'd told Ken I would.

I put a call into Detective Cavanaugh and left a message I didn't expect him to return. No harm in trying. Then I treated myself to a walk through the gardens.

The house looked down over a mile of green lawn edged with broad gardens bearing every type of flowering plant. This ended in a massive quadrangular rose garden with literally hundreds of varieties of roses in full bloom. Magnificent! I joined the line of people strolling down the long hill and took in the colorful displays as I went along. I spent a half hour making my way through this wonderland only to find that the rose garden abutted an orchid conservatory. "Can it get any better than this?" I asked myself. But it did!

After taking in the lush orchids, I found myself at the beginning of yet another garden adventure. By now, the crowds had thinned to a few brave souls. You had to have walked a good forty minutes downhill to get to this point, which meant at least a fifty minute uphill return. There was a plaque at the start of the path indicating I had one mile to go to reach The Lake and The Boathouse.

There was a lake and a boathouse in the garden? That was something I had to see. What was another two miles? I figured I had a good three hours before dark. I'd go for it!

The open path I started on soon turned into a rather narrow trail through the woods. I looked around but didn't see any other visitors. Oh well, the trail would be marked, wouldn't it? It turns out it was, but just barely. At one point, after walking twenty minutes downhill through the woods, I crossed a small wooden bridge over a narrow stream and wondered if I had lost my way. The sign at the start of the path had said The Lake was only a mile away. Surely I'd covered a mile going downhill for twenty minutes! Then, around the next corner, I saw a young couple sitting on an iron bench. Before I could even ask, the young man said, "It's just round the corner, about five minutes ahead."

"Thank you!" I said. "I was beginning to worry."

"No problem," he replied.

I picked up my pace, now more certain of my direction. And sure enough, there it was. A small boat house stood on the other side of a five acre lake. The long wooden bridge that led to the boat house crossed over a spillway. The stream I'd crossed earlier must have been dammed down here to form the Lake. I crossed the bridge and found another wrought iron bench at the side of the boat house. I'd now been walking for an hour since I left the mansion and I was pooped. Sitting down before I started back up that hill sounded like a good idea.

The bench was situated to give a great view of the Lake. Perfect! I settled myself on the bench. Despite being open to the public, this place had an isolated quality to it. A single duck floated on the water. My mind drifted back to Marvin and Brie. How suddenly things could change in life. And death was the ultimate change.

I heard a rustling in the woods behind me. Chills ran down my spine and I shivered and turned. Something moved in the brush about thirty feet from me but it was so dense I couldn't make out what it was. Then I heard voices. A young couple came laughing and running down the path and onto the bridge. They waved to me and I waved back. I decided to walk over and join them.

"Sorry," the young woman said. "We didn't mean to intrude."

"Not at all. I was just heading back up. I nearly lost the trail coming down here so I want to be sure I get back before dusk," I said.

"Why don't you walk back up with us then?" the young man said. "We've been here lots of times."

"Thanks. That would be great," I said. I didn't mind the company one little bit.

We went back up the winding path through the woods and came out at the gardens. It was after 5:00 p.m. by the time we walked back through the gardens to the Biltmore House. Just in time to meet Tissy for cocktails.

Chapter Fifteen

The Visit

I awoke from a nine-hour, deep sleep feeling rested and ready to go. The combination of yesterday's hike, a bit of scotch with dinner, and sleeping without a cat in my bed had worked wonders. As I got ready for the day I thought about my upcoming meeting with Cheryl. I wanted to find out more about her e-mails to Carl and Marvin. An e-mail wasn't much to go on, but neither Ken nor I had come up with any other leads on Marvin's killer.

Detective Cavanaugh had actually returned my call last night but he hadn't been in a talkative mood. "We're working on it Karen. When we have something to say it'll be in the papers," was all he'd said. Geeze! We'd been involved in two other murder investigations together. He could be a bit more communicative! Fine, be that way.

So Cheryl Cushing was the only lead I had.

I drove to Cheryl's home in downtown Asheville. In our brief telephone conversation, Cheryl told me she had sold her country home and moved into town after her husband passed away and their farm had gotten to be too much for her to handle by herself.

I followed the directions she'd given me and parked in front of her house. Cheryl's home was on a pleasant residential street lined with brick homes and mature broad leaf trees. I rang the doorbell and checked out her flower beds while I waited.

Cheryl looked to be in her late sixties. She had a full head of blonde hair which, I was guessing, was courtesy of Clairol. Whatever the source, it looked great on her. Years of sun and life were etched on Cheryl's well tanned skin.

"You must be Karen," she said, opening the front door and greeting me with a ready smile. "Come on in. I was just putting on a pot of green tea. Would you have a cup with me?"

"That sounds great," I said. And indeed it did. I'd acquired a taste for green tea after reading that drinking it everyday would shed pounds without any other change in diet or exercise. Hey, hope springs eternal.

"Come sit in the kitchen with me if you don't mind," Cheryl said, striding ahead of me in her stocking feet. Cheryl had the strong erect carriage of a horse woman.

"This is lovely," I said. The kitchen had full length bay windows that bowed out into Cheryl's abundant floral plantings. You couldn't do better than flowers by me.

"Well, as I said on the phone, I've just moved to the city this year. I fell in love with this house because of the gardens. It reminds me of the ones I had at our farm. After Chet passed away though, I really couldn't keep it all up by myself. Giving up the horses was the hardest part," Cheryl said. She placed the tea pot on the table between the two cups she'd set out for us.

"Did you have many horses?" I asked her.

"Four," Cheryl replied. "I sold three of them to friends that I rode with. But Star was a problem. She'd developed tendonitis last year and really couldn't be ridden," Cheryl said.

"So what did you do with Star?" I asked Cheryl as she poured steaming tea into our cups.

"Well, a trainer I met at a horse show told me he had a client who'd set up a sort of retirement farm for horses. He said Shady Acres, that's the name of the farm, was dedicated to giving horses a safe and caring place to live out their lives when they were too old or injured to be ridden."

"So, you sold Star to Shady Acres?" I asked.

"Oh, no. You really can't sell an injured horse. I paid to have her placed there. Well, not a huge fee, sort of an endowment for her. Not what it would have cost me to board her for the rest of her life, but still, I paid enough to cover Star's expenses for a year or two. It was the least I could do for her," Cheryl said. Tears welled in her eyes.

"You miss her," I said.

"Yes, I do. I'd promised I wouldn't see Star after I gave her up. He said it would be better for Star that way. But then, I kept wondering about her. And the more I thought about it, I didn't see any reason not to call and see how Star was doing. But when I tried, I couldn't find any listing for Shady Acres in Galena. And I couldn't reach Harry. He's probably out of the country on a horse buying trip," Cheryl said. "He takes clients to Europe to find horses every few years."

"Wait a minute, Cheryl. Who is Harry?"

"Harry is the trainer who helped me find a home for Star. You might know him. He's from your area, up there in Galena," Cheryl said.

"He is?" I exclaimed. "Cheryl, what's Harry's full name?"

"Harry Henry," she said. "Do you know him?"

I stared at Cheryl. "I just met a trainer named Harry Henry this weekend. There can't be two of them," I said.

"No, you wouldn't think so," Cheryl said. "If you know Harry, maybe you can help me find Shady Acres. You see, when I couldn't reach Harry, I had the idea to contact the local horse veterinarians up there. I figured one of them had to know Star by now and could tell me how she was doing. I did a search online and found there were only two horse veterinarians in Galena. So I just e-mailed them both," Cheryl said.

"And did you hear back from them?" I asked.

"I heard from one. Marvin Stone. He'd never heard of Shady Acres. Which was odd, I thought. But he did have several new horses in his practice. But no horses named Star. He said he knew Harry, though and he asked me to e-mail him a picture of Star," Cheryl said.

"And did you do that?" I asked.

"Oh, my, yes. Right away."

"When was that, Cheryl?"

"That was just this past Friday," Cheryl replied.

"And did Marvin recognize Star?" I asked, figuring I knew the answer but wanting to hear it directly from Cheryl.

"He said he thought he did, but that her name wasn't Star. It was Goldie. I guess the new owners changed her name for some reason," Cheryl said.

It was all starting to fall into place! Harry hadn't placed Star in a retirement farm. He'd sold her to Brie! Star was Goldie! And Marvin must have confronted Harry with that fact. Maybe Marvin had told Brie as well and Harry had killed them both. I came out of my thoughts to find Cheryl staring at me.

"Are you all right?" Cheryl asked. "You look like you've seen a ghost!"

"I sort of have," I mumbled.

"So, have you seen Star?" Cheryl asked.

"I might have. Cheryl, can I see that picture of Star?" I asked.

"Of course. I have a photo in the living room. Let me get it for you," Cheryl said. She returned with a silver framed photo of a golden brown horse with a white star on its forehead. That cinched it. Star was Goldie.

I had to call Ken—and Detective Cavanaugh.

I left Cheryl around 11:00 a.m. As soon as I got into my car I pulled out my cell phone and called Ken. No answer. Darn! I left a message at his home and on his cell.

Next, I tried Detective Cavanaugh at his office but got his answering machine, too. I left a message and then called right back. This time I got through to the Sheriff Department's receptionist and talked with a real live person. Still, I didn't have any better luck getting through to Cavanaugh himself. I asked the receptionist to pass the message on to Detective Cavanaugh to call me on my cell and left my number. That was about all that I could do for now.

My mind drifted to my conversation with Cheryl. The more I thought about it the more it sounded like Harry must have killed Marvin. And somehow Brie found out and so Harry killed her as well. My forehead tingled. As I rubbed it, I felt a presence and looked around me through the car window. I didn't see anyone and shook the feeling off. I was just spooking myself. I told myself to get a grip and then retraced my way back to the Biltmore Inn. The horse show was already underway and I was set to meet Tissy there at noon.

Chapter Sixteen

The Biltmore Summer Classic Horse Show

Once I was back on the Biltmore Estate I followed the winding, tree-lined road toward the Inn. But this time, I continued on by and followed the signs to the Biltmore Summer Classic Horse Show.

The horse show was located on a long, flat strip of land next to the French Broad River. The river flowed through the valley at the lowest elevation of the estate. As I wound my way down to the horse show, I rode by acres of planted corn fields and chestnut colored cattle grazing in the fenced pastures.

At the bottom of the hillside, a young man in a bright yellow tee-shirt stood at the side of the road and waved me to stop. I rolled down my window and told him I was going to the horse show. He directed me across a narrow, one lane wooden bridge and asked me to drive into the mowed hayfield just beyond the bridge. I made my way cautiously over the bridge and then into the field that had been converted to parking for the week. Two young women were acting as parking directors and they directed me into the next open spot in the long line of trucks, jeeps and cars.

"The shuttle will be along in a few minutes," the taller of the two said.

"Or you can walk," her shorter brunette companion added. "It's just a five minute walk to the show."

"Thanks. I think I will walk," I said and smiled a good-bye. I could see several white tents in the distance and headed out down the dirt road leading from the parking area. The road was level, hard-packed brown dirt. There was a three-foot strip of grass and trees between the road and the French Broad. On my right, through breaks in the trees, I could see the tree-lined far shore about fifty feet away. On my left, the hillside rose, dotted with grassy fields and clusters of tall oak trees. At the very peak of the property, about a mile straight uphill, the Biltmore House looked down over the show.

A golf cart putted past me driven by two teenage girls. They were in their riding gear wearing black knee length boots, tan pants and crisp white blouses. Even sitting in the golf cart they looked strong and athletic. As I approached the first tent I saw that it was an open air canopy covering a raised platform. Several people were seated at the table positioned on the platform. That must be the judges tent, I thought.

Riding rings were delineated by a three-foot tall rail fence. The fence was made out of two-inch by eight-inch wood boards held off the ground by metal posts to form a large rectangular riding arena. Four more golf carts were parked along the perimeter of the riding ring. I guessed these folks were spectators, probably the riders' families. I could see several other white canopies in the distance. There were two rows of riding rings set in a line along the river. This was a much larger scale event than Galena Stables Show.

I stopped at the next ring and took a minute to peruse the booklet the girls in the parking area had given me. The booklet was about thirty pages chock-full of information. It listed the times and qualifications for each division. It looked like the divisions were arranged by categories that were beyond my comprehension. The first ring was titled: "Main Hunter" and listed sixteen different classes such as: Regular Conformation Model, Green Conformation Model, First

Year Green Working Hunter, and Second Year Green Under Saddle. I needed a decoder ring to read this thing.

My eye caught the name of the show I knew was going to be a special feature and I read:

Grand Prix Classes.

Class Conditions for 601 & 602: National Standard. To be conducted and scored under Table II.2.a. ALL HORSES MUST BE ON THE SHOW GROUNDS 24 HOURS PRIOR TO THE CLASS TO COMPLY WITH THE 24 HOUR RULE. Horses not on the grounds prior to that time will not be able to compete.

Order of Go: All horses showing in class 601-602 must be declared 24 hours prior to the class.

Poling: Absolutely no poling or offsets are allowed at any time.

Attire: Formal attire required.

Awards: Winners to ride for presentation of awards. Trophy and ribbons 1-12.

Prize Money: $7,500, $3,250, $2,000, $1,500, $1,250, $1,000, $750, $750, $500, $500, $500.

Each Grand Prix held at this show is eligible for inclusion on the USEF Computer List.

There were a lot of defined terms which obviously had significance to the riders even though I had no idea what they meant. Wait a minute, the old lawyer in me said. I can figure this out. I flipped the page and came to the Rules and Regulations section of the book. Ten pages of small type set out the rules for everything from stabling, to competitors' attire, to rules for the dogs at the show (they must be on a leash), to Night Watch. I read the Night Watch paragraph and learned that all horses occupying a stall are checked six times per night each night of the show. Wow, that's a lot of checking. But I guess these were pretty valuable horses. I skimmed the rest of the booklet and saw advertisements for nurseries, stables, golf carts, show jumps, and a full page ad for something to tune your truck's engine to tow horse trailers. Interesting to see the sorts of things I'd never heard of that you need for a horse show. It was quite another world.

Before I'd had a chance to read more, I was jarred from my reverie by a familiar voice, "Karen!"

I looked up to see Tissy waving and walking towards me. Tissy's involved with organizing the horse show and handles all of the stabling reservations. In fact, it was Tissy that invited Bella to cater the Grand Prix dinner.

"Tissy!" I called back and hurried towards her. We welcomed each other with a hug and a laugh. "How's the show going?" I asked.

"Excellent! Great turn out and gorgeous weather. Couldn't ask for anything more!" Tissy said.

"Let me get you a golf cart. Come on back with me to the office," Tissy said.

"No, no. I'm fine walking," I said.

"I've got my golf cart all ready and waiting for you. You'll be glad you have it after a few hours, believe me!" Tissy said. "This place is bigger than you think! Come on, it's parked right back there," Tissy said, pointing to the next ring down.

"All right," I said. "I'm sure you're right!" We walked together to Tissy's golf cart and hopped in. Tissy started it up with a turn of the key and we bounced along on the grass over to the dirt road. We passed two more riding rings and a large, enclosed white tent with an adjoining canopied area.

"That's the food tent," Tissy said. As we jetted by I could see white tables and chairs with groups of riders eating lunch. "My office is in there," Tissy said, indicating a trailer at the far edge of the show area. "Let me give you a little tour before I give you the golf cart."

"Sounds great! Thanks," I said.

We continued along the same hard packed dirt road with the French Broad River meandering to our right. Just beyond the office trailers Tissy said, "That's the shopping area. We can stop and walk through there on our way back."

"There's a shopping area?" I asked, surprised.

"Sure. There's clothing, riding gear and beautiful jewelry. The artist who designed and painted the cover of our program and our posters has a booth there, too. I'll bet you'd enjoy meeting her," Tissy said.

"I'd love to do that," I said.

We continued down the road moving away from the show area. Another trailer was parked just off the road and Tissy said, "That's our blacksmith's trailer. The horse stalls are just ahead there."

The layout for the show was similar to the Galena Stables' Show but on a much larger scale. There were at least four times as many horse stalls and the landscaping around them was gorgeous.

"Now, just past here, is the mobile home area," Tissy said.

We must have covered about a mile on our tour at this point. Dozens of large mobile homes were parked in rows. I chuckled as I saw one with an inflatable swimming pool filled with water. A little dog was sitting next to the pool and I wondered if it was for him. Tissy must have read my mind because she said, "That's Ox's trailer. His family travels together to the shows. In fact, there's Mary now."

"Hey, Tissy," a woman in her thirties waved to us with her free hand. A toddler clung to her other hand and wobbled along next to her.

"Hey, Mary," Tissy replied as she stopped the cart. "Let me introduce you to Karen."

"Hi, Mary," I said.

"We're just finishing our tour and heading to the food tent for a little lunch."

"The burgers are excellent," Mary said. "Ox and I had lunch there a little earlier."

"We'll give them a try," Tissy said and waved good-bye as we continued on our tour.

"So, that's our world here," Tissy said. "Let's grab a bite to eat and then I'll head over and get set up for the Grand Prix tonight."

"What time does that start?" I asked.

"Six p.m. sharp," Tissy said. "We've got a place reserved for you at our table," she added.

We drove back past the trailers and the tented horse stalls. Lots of people meandered around. Grooms led horses and young riders walked together. Golf carts buzzed by and several were parked outside the office trailer.

We continued on over to the riding area and parked the golf cart at the edge of the large white food tent next to a half dozen other golf carts. The smell of burgers filled the air. An announcer's voice drifted to us from the adjacent riding ring, "Next, Number 298, Wanda Brio on Doctor's Orders."

The announcer's voice faded as we walked into the shade of the food tent. There were fifteen or twenty tables draped with white table cloths. A central table held silverware, napkins and assorted drinks. At the head of the tent was a buffet and ordering line. As I walked up to take a peek at the buffet a familiar voice called my name.

"Karen!" Bella called from the working side of the buffet. Dressed in a white chef's toque and jacket, Bella looked even more imposing than usual. She came around the buffet line and gave Tissy and me a hug.

"We were just going to have some of your great lunch. Any chance you can join us?" Tissy asked.

"I could use a little lunch break," Bella said. "Marge, you can handle things for a while, right?" Bella said more than asked the young woman in a white coat who stood behind the counter.

"Sure," Marge replied.

"If anything comes up, I'll be at the table back there," Bella added.

We made our way through the buffet and settled into the farthest table still in the shade. I looked around and noticed nearly half the diners had canine companions.

"What do you hear from Ken?" Bella asked. "Any news?"

I filled Bella in on what I'd learned from Cheryl Cushing. "You'd better be careful," Tissy said.

"Me, what do you mean?" I asked.

"If that fellow's devious enough to sell a bad horse, no telling what else he'd do," she said.

"Well, no one knows I met with her, except Ken and Detective Cavanaugh, so I think I'm safe," I said. But I remembered the sensation of someone watching me by the Boathouse yesterday afternoon and then again as I left Cheryl's this morning. I was just getting goosey, I thought.

After we finished lunch, Bella and Tissy went back to their respective roles with the horse show. I sat alone for a few minutes, taking in the sights and sounds. Just as I was getting up to leave, I noticed a solitary, rather large man in jeans and a cowboy hat staring at me from across the tented dining area. He looked vaguely familiar and I nodded but he turned away. My forehead tingled and I thought he must be one of the trainers I'd met at Galena Stables. He could have been—but he wasn't. He was the fellow Lynne and I saw talking to Norman Trout by the old brewery! I almost hadn't recognized him in this context. What was he doing here?

Chapter Seventeen

Grand Prix

The afternoon went by in a flash. I watched the Hunter classes and met some very interesting people, including a neat lady named Chris. Chris explained that the Hunter rings were made to resemble jumping conditions hunters on horseback might encounter in the hunt field: hedges, fences, a few subtle flowers. The Hunter classes had eight fences made of brown painted wood. Several had red brick pillars, rather like gate pillars, holding the boards. Green shrubs decorated the base of each jump. The Hunters were judged on their form over jumps. I watched the show for several hours and then decided to fit in a quick tour of the Biltmore winery. I had just buzzed back to the Inn for a quick change. I looked at my watch and it was already 5:30 p.m. Yikes! The Grand Prix started at 6:00 p.m. and I got there just ten minutes before it started.

I parked the car and this time I caught the shuttle to the Grand Prix area. There were hundreds of people there awaiting the show. The canopied tent where dinner would be served required a special admission ticket. As I made my way into the tent I saw why. Large silver platters of beef roast, a variety of salads and vegetables, rolls and a scrumptious looking lemon tart filled the buffet. It all looked wonderful. I was getting hungry looking at this delectable array. Long tables covered with white table cloths were decorated with baskets of flowering pink petunias.

I found my assigned table and was the first one there. Phew. So much for worrying about being late! Our table had an excellent view of the Grand Prix ring. The ring was about the size of a football field. There were at least twelve brightly painted wooden jumps in the ring and they looked a lot higher than the ones I'd seen this afternoon. The Grand Prix featured the Jumpers. The overall impression of this ring was bright and highly decorated in comparison to the Hunter rings. The Jumper jumps were brightly painted red, white and yellow boards with extravagant floral plantings.

Several formally dressed riders walked the ring and studied the course. Other riders sat on their horses or stood next to them just outside the ring.

A large digital display sign flickered to life at one end of the ring. I noticed there were two judges in the judging booth and an announcer on an elevated stand at the far end of the ring. I studied the show booklet at my table and read the scoring rules for the Grand Prix. It read:

While the Grand Prix course may be complex, the nature of the competition is simple and easy to follow. The object is for a horse to clear every obstacle in the course with the lowest number of faults or penalties. The competitor with the fewest faults and the fastest time wins. Scoring is determined as follows:

> *First disobedience (refusal to jump fence)...............4 faults*
>
> *Second disobedience...Elimination*
>
> *Knockdown of an obstacle (touches do not count).........4 faults*
>
> *Any foot in Liverpool, water, or tape ....4 faults*
>
> *Fall of horse or rider ....Elimination*
>
> *Exceeding the time allowed for first round...1 fault per second*
>
> *Exceeding the time allowed in jump off......1 fault per second*

Off course... Elimination

O.K. That doesn't sound too complicated. Not too complicated to watch, that is. Doing it would be another matter. I had a great deal of respect for the skill, discipline and just plain guts of these riders.

Just then, Tissy and a group of her fellow horse people joined me at our table. Tissy introduced me to the other seven guests who, it turned out, were horse folks from Chicago. We had fun playing "Six degrees of Separation" and learned we had several friends in common, including Polly Andrews. Dara Brown and Sassie Ballantine joined us just as we were making our way to the buffet table. We returned to our table just in time for the start of the Grand Prix.

Trumpets blared to signal the opening ceremonies. We all stood for the singing of the national anthem and then the show began.

"Our first rider on course is Madeline Stewart on Rainmaker." A gorgeous chestnut horse entered the ring. The rider wore formal riding attire including black velvet riding helmet, pink oxford blouse, black riding jacket, stretchy tan riding pants and knee-high black leather riding boots. She sat high in her saddle as she made her circle and then leaned forward as she took the first jump. "Flawless" the fellow sitting next to me said. Madeline cantered her horse to the next jump. The horse leapt forward, tucking its front legs as they passed over the hurdle. The horse seemed to take the fence in liquid motion. Rainmaker extended his powerful legs, landed and continued cantering forward. The third jump was flawless as well. The crowd was riveted as Rainmaker took the fourth, fifth and sixth jumps. Then Madeline and Rainmaker approached the next to final and tallest jump. A sigh of disappointment rose from the crowd as the horse's rear hoof clipped the top rail, rocking it, and sending it tumbling to the ground. The rider valiantly continued, although her chances of winning had most probably crashed along with that rail.

"A rail at the next to last fence for Madeline Stewart resulting in four faults," the announcer said. "And now for our next rider, Boo

Bellington, on Winged Victory." The crowd applauded as Boo rode into the ring. Boo was the first male competitor I'd watched ride. He was dressed in a red riding jacket, tan pants, and black boots and helmet. He cut a stunning figure on his gorgeous pure black horse. "Interesting that his horse is named for the statue in the Louvre," I said to Jason, my dinner companion seated to my right.

"Boo's into art as well as horses," Jason replied.

Boo picked up a canter and maneuvered the course brilliantly. "A clean round for Boo Bellington," the announcer said as the crowd applauded. This was getting to be interesting.

Twenty-four more riders competed in the first round of the Grand Prix. Then the announcer said there were six riders clean for the jump-off. This was the equivalent of a play-off. While the course was changed for the jump off, I asked Tissy about the arrangement of the course. She explained that there are two general types of fences: a vertical fence and a spread fence. The spread fence has two bars at the top which, as the name implies, are spread apart. The degree of difficulty is a function of the height, spread and placement in relation to the other jumps on the course. In this level of competition, there are also walls which are solid obstacles usually four to eight feet tall, and a water jump.

"Watching these horses and riders take those jumps is absolutely awe-inspiring," Dara said.

In the jump-off, as Boo approached the final fence, his horse balked. A collective sigh went up from the crowd. Boo made a tight circle with his horse and then took the last jump flawlessly. But the horse's refusal cost Boo four faults and time. Mary Ellen Chove completed the jump off with a clean round and the fastest time. There was a ribbon and trophy presentation, the winner taking home a check for $7,500. Second place took a red ribbon and a check for $3,250. Not bad for either of them!

"There's a dance after dinner," Tissy told me. "I hope you can stay.

"I'm planning on it," I said. "I think I'll take a stroll while the band's getting ready. I want to take one last look at the Biltmore Gardens. I head out bright and early tomorrow morning. You don't mind do you?" I asked.

"Of course not. Music starts at 8:00 and goes until 10:00 tonight. So, I'll see you back here then," Tissy said.

"Would either of you like to join me?" I asked Dara and Sassie.

"No, thanks. I'd like to stay here and visit a bit," Dara said.

"Me too. There are a lot of folks I'd like to catch up with," Sassie said.

"I'll see you all back here at 8:00 then," I said and headed for the shuttle back up to the mansion.

When I exited the shuttle at the Biltmore House, there was a sign saying the gardens were open to the public until 9 p.m. That meant I'd have plenty of time for my stroll. I made my way around to the back of the mansion, down the garden-lined grassy hill, to the rose garden. The evening air was filled with fragrant rose perfume. There weren't many tourists this time of day so I practically had the gardens to myself.

I made my way to the path leading down to the lake and the boathouse. It had been a strenuous hike yesterday, but that lake was so pretty. And I figured I'd know my way this time. In fact, it seemed much easier and quicker today. At the bottom of the trail I walked across the narrow wooden bridge and sat on the bench overlooking the lake. I enjoyed the quiet atmosphere. The warm late-afternoon sun reflected off the water. A slight breeze tickled the treetops. Then I heard footsteps on the bridge. As the figure got closer, I recognized Harry Henry! Uh-oh. What was he doing here? Did he know I knew about Cheryl? How could he? "Calm down," I told myself. My heart raced. Adrenaline pumped through my veins. I tried to convince myself that this was just a coincidence. He'd probably just come here for a little tour after the Horse Show, just like I had. Yeah, right. He was three-quarters of the way across the bridge when I saw his gun. I scanned the area for another path out of here—an escape route. There wasn't one. The trail ended here. The boathouse next to me was small and padlocked. My choices were limited: jump into the lake, hide in the woods, make a mad dash past Harry on the narrow bridge, or just sit here and pretend I didn't know a thing.

"Karen, I see you've been visiting Cheryl Cushing. You really should have kept your nose out of this," Harry said as he stepped off the bridge. So much for the "just pretend I didn't know" option. I dashed behind the rickety boathouse. It wasn't much, but if I could keep this wooden structure between us maybe I could work my way back around it to the path and make a dash for it back up the hill. I'd have to stay ahead of him and I figured I'd have a better chance on a clear path than I would crashing through the woods. I had a possibility of running into another tourist on the path, slim as that possibility might be at this time of day.

Suddenly a shot rang out! I ducked. A gaping hole appeared in the boathouse two feet from my shoulder. I ducked instinctively and tip-toed to the corner of the boathouse. This was like Russian roulette!

I couldn't just stay here. That was a death trap for sure. I took a deep breath, exhaled and peeked around the corner. The bridge was only ten feet away. I slipped around the corner of the boathouse just as another shot rang out.

"No point in running, Karen," Harry said in a low voice. But run I did, faster than I'd ever run before. My foot hit the wooden bridge and slid. I heard another shot as I hit the deck of the bridge. The fall knocked the air out of my lungs. I looked up to see Roger Lesser coming out of the woods by the boathouse with a gun in his hand —and it was pointed right at me!

"What? What are you doing here?" I stammered, gasping for breath.

"You're about to find out," Roger said. "Get up off that bridge and get back behind the boathouse," he commanded.

Since the gun was pointed at me, I didn't have much choice but to do as he said. I scrambled to my feet and dusted off my pants.

"Never mind that! Get going!" he said again.

I walked slowly back the way I'd come half expecting Harry Henry to show up any second with his gun pointed at me, too. "So, you and Harry Henry are in this together?" I asked, as I walked as slowly as I could. I didn't expect anything good to be waiting for me behind that boathouse. But I hadn't expected what I saw next. Harry Henry lay face down, blood oozing through his shirt. He'd been shot dead.

"So, you see, Harry and I are not quite in this together. The fool! He thought he could blackmail me! Two-bit little hustler is all he ever was!" Roger said.

"Blackmail you? What would he blackmail you about?" I asked.

"So, you're curious even now? Right before you die? O.K. It can't hurt to tell you before I shoot you! You see, Harry saw me cut the rip cord on Marvin's parachute. The parachute was right there in Marvin's van parked next to the stable. It was easy to cut the rip cord and tuck the end back in so Marvin wouldn't notice it."

"But why did you do it? Why did you want to kill Marvin in the first place?" I asked.

"Unfortunately for Marvin, he overheard me talking to one of my dealers. You see, I have a very lucrative side business. I knew Marvin was going to tell the police and I had to stop him."

"So you cut the parachute cord to make it look like an accident?" I asked.

"I know enough about parachutes from my days in the Army to realize that any good investigation would show the pull cord had been cut. They'd know it wasn't an accident. That's why I had to kill Brie. Everyone would think she killed Marvin and then killed herself. It was perfect, except for Harry finding out and getting greedy," Roger said.

"So you shot Harry to shut him up and prevent him from blackmailing you."

"Exactly. And now I'm going to shoot you with Harry's gun. When the police find you here it will look like you and Harry shot each other. I'll make sure the police learn about Harry's horse swindling deal. It'll look like he shot you to stop you from telling people about his horse dealings with Cheryl Cushing and Brie. And, I'll plant the gun I used to shoot Harry on you so that it looks like you shot Harry in self-defense. Unfortunately, you'll be dead. So, enough talk. Get over there by Harry. That's where I'm going to shoot you!"

Chapter Eighteen

To Friends

"Police! Get down!" someone yelled. I wasn't going to argue, I hit the ground fast and looked up to see a man, gun drawn, running toward us across the bridge. It was Cavanaugh!

"Karen, stay down!" he yelled again. I rolled to the wooded side of the path. Cavanaugh ran past me. Two uniformed Asheville policemen were right behind him.

"He's behind the boathouse," I yelled pointing to where Roger Lesser had just run.

Three more shots sounded in quick succession. Then there was silence—dead silence.

Detective Cavanaugh came over to me and helped me up. The thought of how close I'd just come had my mind whirling. "Thank you!" I said. "But how did you know I was here?"

"You were lucky there. You see, I followed Roger out of the horse show and Roger was following Harry. And it turned out, Harry was following you."

"But how did you know about Roger?" I asked.

"Norman Trout was the key. Remember when I told you there was a major meth dealer in the area that Norman was tracking? Well,

Norman finally met the fellow and it turned out to be Roger Lesser. He was selling methamphetamine as a quick way to make money. His manufacturing company had been losing money for him for years. But that's how he laundered his drug money," Detective Cavanaugh said.

"When did the Asheville police get involved?" I asked.

"You see, I knew Roger was coming down here for the Horse Show. So, when Norman pegged Roger as the drug dealer, I called the Asheville police and had them follow Roger. Then I caught the first plane down here myself," Detective Cavanaugh explained. "In the meantime, Harry had staked out Cheryl's house to see if she was alone. He was planning to confront her and scare her into keeping quiet about the horse deal. But when you arrived, Karen, Harry realized he had to silence you first. When you left the horse show he saw his chance. He followed you, Roger followed him, and since we were following Roger, that led us to you," Detective Cavanaugh said.

"Lucky for me," I said.

"Yes, indeed," Detective Cavanaugh said. Two more uniformed police officers came across the bridge. "I'm going to the Asheville police station with these officers. There's going to be a lot of paperwork with two people shot dead here. And I want to make sure our departments are coordinated on this."

"Can I go back to the horse show?" I asked.

"I'll tell you what. I'll take you back up there myself, then we can go to the station and give our statements together," Detective Cavanaugh said.

Fifteen minutes later, Tissy, Detective Cavanaugh, Dara, Sassie and I sat around a table at the Exhibitors' party. The Biltmore House was lit now and glowed against the evening sky. The horse show folks were all here celebrating a great horse show and a wonderful life. Detective Cavanaugh and I were, once again, celebrating still being here at all.

Tissy raised her glass, "To our all being here to enjoy this!"

"To our all being here," I repeated, with emphasis. We clinked our glasses and took a sip of champagne.

"I'd like to make a special toast, "To Detective Cavanaugh. Thank you," I said.

"Yes, indeed," Tissy said. "I heard the rescue story! But why did Roger kill Harry? Was Harry involved in the drug dealing?" Tissy asked.

"No, Harry was a horse swindler but not a drug dealer. Harry had sold Brie a lame horse then drugged it, at least until the deal was closed," Detective Cavanaugh said. "But Harry thought he'd figured out another way to make some easy money. He tried to blackmail Roger. And that turned out to be Harry's fatal mistake," Detective Cavanaugh said.

"What was Harry using to blackmail Roger?" Dara asked.

"Harry saw Roger in Marvin's van that Fourth of July morning at Galena Stables. Harry didn't realize that Roger was cutting Marvin's parachute rip cord until after Marvin had crashed. But afterward, Harry put two and two together and he decided to blackmail Roger instead of tell the police," Detective Cavanaugh said.

"But why did Roger want to kill Marvin in the first place?" Dara asked.

"It was a crime of opportunity. That Saturday morning, Roger met with one of his drug dealers at Galena Stables. It was early, 6:00 a.m. and Roger didn't think anyone else was around. But Marvin was there doing his rounds. Marvin was there earlier than usual so he could get ready for his balloon jump. I don't know whether Roger and Marvin had words or not, but Marvin left an urgent message on my answering machine saying that he wanted to see me right after his jump. In the message told me he'd seen someone selling drugs at the stable. Of course, he never got the chance to tell me who he'd seen," Detective Cavanaugh said.

"How did Roger know enough about parachutes to cut that cord?" Tissy asked.

"My background check on Roger showed he'd been in the Army in his twenties. He got his parachute training back then," Detective Cavanaugh said.

"Wasn't Roger taking a chance that someone would see him in Marvin's van?" I asked.

"There weren't many people at Galena Stables that early in the morning. And besides, he could always say he was waiting for Marvin," Detective Cavanaugh said.

"But what about Brie? Did Harry kill her because she found out about his lame horse deal?" Tissy asked.

"We found Roger's DNA on the syringe used to inject the lethal dose of drugs into Brie. Roger thought everyone would assume Brie had killed Marvin and then taken the drugs herself. Her past drug use was common knowledge," Detective Cavanaugh said.

"So Roger planned to have it look like Brie had killed Marvin," I said.

"Roger planted the knife he'd used to cut the parachute rip cord in Brie's stable. But we traced the knife and found Roger had bought the knife from The Knife Store in Galena just two months ago," Detective Cavanaugh said. "So, we've got him on the drug dealing and the art theft, too," Detective Cavanaugh said.

"The art theft!" Tissy and I said simultaneously.

"Yes, once we had Roger pegged as the murderer, we got a warrant to search his business and his home. We found the two paintings, Lynne Shaw's Caitlin and Liz Seelig's Heade, stashed away in a secret closet in his office at the telephone factory," Detective Cavanaugh said.

"Good heavens," I said. "I'll bet they were both glad to get their paintings back."

"Yes, especially Liz. She hadn't had time to insure the Heade. She'd only found out its value at the Antique Art Show," Detective Cavanaugh said.

"Yes, and Roger was there so he knew its value," I said.

"But why did Roger want the painting? Do you think he was going to sell it?" Tissy asked.

"Drug dealers have started using valuable paintings as collateral for drug deals. Roger probably saw his chance to use those paintings to buy other drugs and expand his dealing," Detective Cavanaugh said.

"You're kidding!" Dara exclaimed.

"Oh, you're right! I just read a book about that! They've been doing that for years now. It started with radical political groups in Ireland taking paintings from country estates and holding them for ransom. They'd use the ransom money to buy weapons. With all the press some of the recent art auctions have gotten, the criminal element realized that art had verifiable value. Someone who wanted to buy drugs could steal a painting and use it for collateral for a drug buy. The seller would hold the painting as collateral for payment for the drugs. That way the drug buyer could resell the drugs and use the proceeds to redeem the painting. Sort of a collateralized financial arrangement among drug dealers," I said.

"But you got the paintings back safe and sound, didn't you?" Tissy asked.

"Yes, we did," Detective Cavanaugh said.

"Oh, in all this I almost forgot! This afternoon I saw another drug dealer here at the horse show! The fellow Lynne and I saw threaten Norman Trout is here!" I gasped.

"We know. We picked him up, too. The Asheville police have him in custody along with his boss, Roger Lesser," Detective Cavanaugh said.

"Here's to you," I said, raising my glass.

"To you both," Tissy said.

"All's well that ends well," Sassie said over the clink of our glasses.

"Let's have another toast. To Friends," I said.

"To Friends," Tissy, Dara, Sassie and Detective Cavanaugh said.

The five of us raised our glasses and clinked their rims again. The high tone of crystal rang strong and clear.

We all took another sip of champagne. It was good to be alive. I couldn't wait to call Ken and tell him what had happened. This might just be the perfect time for that trip to St. Barth's we've been talking about. We could both use a nice quiet vacation on a beautiful Caribbean island. I think we just might do that!

.

The End—for now.

Bella's Best Recipes

Peaches in Red Wine Sauce

6 fresh peaches
1 cup sugar
2 cups full bodied red wine such as a Chianti Classico, Merlot or
Cabernet

Wash, dry, and slice the peaches in half lengthwise.

Remove the pit and slice peach halves lengthwise into thin slices.

Place peach slices in a bowl and sprinkle with sugar. Stir gently to
coat peaches.

Cover peaches with the red wine.

Stir again gently until sugar is dissolved.

Allow the peaches to marinate one hour at room temperature.

Spoon peaches and wine sauce into stemmed glass ware, and serve
immediately.

Serves 6

Roasted Vegetables

1 ¼ cup olive oil
3 cloves garlic
1 teaspoon oregano
1 teaspoon salt
½ teaspoon pepper
1 tablespoon crushed rosemary
1 teaspoon rubbed sage
2 Fennel Bulbs
4 young zucchini
3 young eggplants
5 tomatoes, cut in half
3 onions
1 head cauliflower

Pour olive oil into a large baking dish.
Peel and crush garlic. Add the garlic to the olive oil in the baking dish.
Add oregano, salt and pepper to the olive oil.
Crush rosemary leaves and add to olive oil.
 Rub sage leaves and add to the olive oil.
Stir olive oil and spices to mix together.
Wash, dry and quarter 2 fennel bulbs and place in the baking dish.
Wash, dry and slice zucchini into long strips. Add to baking dish.
Wash, dry and slice eggplant into ½ inch rounds. Add to baking dish.
Wash, dry and slice tomatoes in half. Add to baking dish.
Peel onions and cut in half. Add to baking dish.
Wash, dry and quarter cauliflower. Add to baking dish.
Stir vegetables gently to coat with the seasoned olive oil.
Cover baking dish containing all vegetables and marinate at room temperature for one hour. Stir occasionally to be sure all vegetables are marinated.
Place covered baking dish in 450 degree oven for 30 minutes, or until vegetables are tender.
 Serves 8

Roasted Italian Beef

2 ½ pound beef roast (boneless bottom roast)
2 garlic cloves
1/8 cup olive oil
1 sprig rosemary
1 sprig oregano
1 sprig basil
3 stalks parsley
Salt and pepper to taste

Preheat oven to 350 degrees. Rinse roast and place it in a deep roasting pan. Peel the garlic and cut the cloves in half lengthwise. Make small slits in the roast and slip the garlic cloves into the slits. Rub the roast with the olive oil.

Sprinkle the roast with the rosemary, oregano and basil leaves, crushing the herbs with your fingers as you sprinkle. Coarsely chop the parsley leaves and sprinkle the roast with the parsley leaves, salt and pepper.

Roast the meat whole in a covered pan until the meat reaches an internal temperature of 160 degrees. This will take approximately one hour.

Remove the roast from the pan and let it cool. Reserve the juices from the pan. Deglaze the pan with ½ cup beef bullion, and add to reserved juices. Wrap the roast in saran wrap. Refrigerate roast and reserved juices overnight.

Slice cold roast into thin slices, cutting meat against the grain. Return the sliced meat to the roasting pan. Add the reserved juices. Bake at 200 degrees until the meat is tender, approximately two hours.
Serve hot, on a crusty bun, with the juice.

Serves 6

Amaretti Cookies

8 ounce can almond paste
1 cup granulated sugar
2 large egg whites
¼ cup granulated sugar for topping

Preheat oven to 375 degrees.

Place sugar in Cuissinart and pulse for 30 seconds until very fine.

Add almond paste, by spoonfuls, to the sugar in Cuissinart. Pulse to mix.

Add egg whites 1/3 at a time, pulsing after each addition.

Mix well, about1 minute.

Drop spoonfuls of dough in ball shape onto well greased cookie sheet. You may use parchment paper to make removing cookies easier.

Bake at 375 degrees for 15 minutes, until cookies puff up and are golden brown.

Remove from pan and let cool.

Serves 12

Makes about 36 amaretti cookies.

Mailing List

To receive your notice of the next Karen Prince Mystery
Send your name and address to:

Galena Publishing
PO Box 18
Galena, IL 61036

Or e-mail: skprincipe@aol.com. You can send your e-mail
address if you would prefer to be notified electronically.

You can use this page, or a copy of it:

Name:_____

**Street
Address:**_____

City, State and Zip code:_____

E-mail Address: _____

Autographed Copies

of

Murder at Galena Stables

Murder on the Mississippi

and **Murder in Galena**

Buy online at: www.sandraprincipe.com

Or use this

MAIL ORDER FORM

Please send me:

_____ autographed copies of Murder at Galena Stables

_____ autographed copies of Murder on the Mississippi

_____ autographed copies of Murder in Galena

I enclose $15.50 for each copy. Please make check payable to: Galena Publishing.

Shipping Charges are $2.50 per book.

Please add 6.25% sales tax if shipped to an Illinois address.

Send my books to:

Name: _____

Street Address: _____

City and State: _____

Zip Code: _____

Mail this form to: **Galena Publishing**

PO Box 18

Galena, IL 61036

About the Author

Sandra Principe lives with her husband in the countryside near Galena. A Chicago lawyer for 20 years, she moved to the Galena area in 1996 to write and paint. She received her Bachelor of Science in English Education and her Juris Doctorate Degree from the University of Wisconsin, Madison.

Ms. Principe's paintings have been shown in galleries and museums across the country from Florida to California. This novel is a unique combination of her special knowledge of Galena, painting and mysteries. Ms. Principe's first mystery, Murder in Galena, was published in 2003. Her second mystery, Murder on the Mississippi, was published in 2005. This is the third book in the Karen Prince Galena Mystery Series.

See Sandra Principe's paintings and learn more about her work at: **www.sandraprincipe.com**